# THE
# WOLF SHIFTER'S
# REDEMPTION

## Also by Amanda Reid

*The Flannigan Sisters Mysteries* Cozy Mystery Novellas

Finders Keepers

Ghosts, Pies, & Alibis

Murder Most Merry

# The Enchanted Rock Immortals World

*The Wolf Shifter's Redemption* by Amanda Reid

# THE
# WOLF SHIFTER'S REDEMPTION

An Enchanted Rock Novella

## AMANDA REID

ISBN: 978-1-951770-03-7

*For Eve, Fenley, Robin and Susan.*

# THE ENCHANTED ROCK IMMORTALS

**Demons and Vampires. Elves and Fairies. Mages and Witches. Werewolves and Dragons. Psychics and Telekinetics.**

These magical beings and more exist, rubbing shoulders in their daily lives with unsuspecting humans. But a supernatural society doesn't happen without order. Millennia ago, the Clans —Sanguis, Fae, Magic, Shifter, and Human Paranormal— wisely formed a Council to maintain that order. The end? To ensure the worlds of human and paranormal beings didn't collide and break out into a war that would result in the extermination or subjugation of either.

As human civilization progressed, the first council formed the All Clan Charter at the natural vortex in Great Zimbabwe, giving each clan a voice in the administration of affairs both between the clans and with humans. Next, Asia formed its council at Chengtu Vortex. Then European at Warel Chakra Vortex. North America came next at the natural vortex humans called Enchanted Rock, in what today is known as Texas.

Now, thriving communities of paranormal beings exist in

and around the granite outcropping. Humans scrabble over the dome, not suspecting an entire city exists within its confines: the North American Council and all its departments—Legislative, Administrative, Security, Medical, Vortex Transportation, and Legal, plus restaurants, clan hotels, and shops catering to the paranormal crowds.

Also under that dome? Intrigue, politics, and most importantly, love.

These are the stories of The Enchanted Rock Immortals.

# CHAPTER 1

What a time for her truck's air conditioning to go out. August. Hottest damn time of the year in Texas.

Wind blasted through the open windows. Carrie Fletcher kept the steering wheel steady with her knees while she threaded her ponytail through the hole in the back of her feed store gimme cap. She tugged the brim down to sit firm on her forehead. A tendril of hair worked its way into her mouth. She spit the strand out and tucked it behind her ear.

At least her border collie, Max, didn't mind the open windows. The pup's black and white freckled front legs stood on the armrest and her ears flapped in the wind. Max turned her head to look at Carrie, tongue lolling from a huge doggie grin as her white-tipped, feathery tail waved from side to side.

Excitement bubbled through Carrie's mind. The source? Max, who enjoyed all the smells from the open window. "You're welcome." Carrie eased the window up a bit with the electronic switch to keep her best friend from toppling out.

Max didn't seem to care. Her nose went back to sucking as

many odors as her nostrils could get from the summer-burnt Central Texas pastures flying by.

The canine happiness couldn't keep the pressing problem at bay. Barry said the last time he repaired her A/C it had been merely a patch. Now that it pooped out again, she had to put the truck in Barry's shop for at least a day. Maybe more. And as a mobile vet, she couldn't afford the downtime plus a whole new compressor. If she had a stationary office it would be doable, but she towed her practice behind her in a sixteen-foot tricked-out trailer.

Unless... She could do a free spay and neuter clinic. Write it off on taxes. It wouldn't be immediate, but at least she could get a break in what she owed the IRS. And for the immediate amount, she'd just have to bring her lunch for the month instead of stopping for a mid-day bite at a drive-thru.

Another bead of sweat slipped between her breasts to be absorbed by her already soaked sports bra. *Gah.* She needed A/C. If Barry would let her hold the clinic in his parking lot, spay and neuter event it was.

Old Man Brigger's house passed in her peripheral vision, heralding her destination, Split, one of the largely-paranormal communities surrounding Enchanted Rock. Human Paranormals, like her, and lesser fae comprised most of the tiny population. She knew almost everyone and everyone her.

The reduced speed sign appeared over the rise. The hood of Deputy Ecker's patrol car didn't peek out from behind the Newberry's dilapidated barn, but she slowed down to fifty-five, then thirty-five, from sheer habit.

Two stoplights, a left, and then a block behind Main Street, she pulled into Barry's Auto Repair. Her gaze slipped to the clock on her dash. Whew. Five minutes to closing. She pulled her truck and its trailer to a halt, but let the diesel engine idle. She wouldn't be long.

With Max trotting at her side, she strode through the closest open bay door. Since Barry hated paperwork as much as a calf getting neutered, odds were he'd be performing surgery on a car rather than hanging out in his office. Thick, stubby legs poked out from under the front end of a sedan.

Bingo.

"Carrie!" Barry Montez slid from underneath a car. He wiped his hands on an oil-stained rag, then stuffed it in the back pocket of his jeans and jumped up with relative ease, considering his bulk. People might mistake his short stature and roundness for fat. But she'd seen him go gremlin on what had to be a half-elf who once tried to give him bewitched counterfeit money. Why they considered gremlins lesser fae, she'd never comprehend. That punk still probably felt the beating Barry laid on him two months ago.

The gremlin pulled his ball cap's brim from back to front and tugged it down over the grizzled ring of gray hair on his head. He held out his hand. "A/C out again?"

Though she'd washed her hands, where they'd been today couldn't have been worse than his. She clasped the outstretched palm. "Wish it was a social visit. I need the compressor fixed."

His lips twisted. "I can get it ordered today, probably will come in late tomorrow, and I'll start Thursday morning. Should be done that afternoon. Same price I quoted."

Rats. Two more days until it was fixed. "Sounds good. I'll see you Thursday morning then." She scanned the empty lot across the street. A broad, shady oak tree covered one part, someone had mowed the grass. "Who owns that lot over there?"

"Me. Use it as an overflow."

"Can I set up a free spay-neuter clinic while you're installing the compressor?" She'd have to rearrange her appointments, since she couldn't be a mobile vet without being mobile. "The free day can allow me to help out some Splitters. It'll be an initial outlay, but it'll help with taxes on the back end."

His face lit up. Money was something a gremlin understood. "Sure. You need any help? MayLee's been talking about going to school to be a vet. She's always changing her mind, that's why I didn't bring it up before. But for the last six months she's watched those vet shows on TV." He shook his head. "If helping spay or neuter doesn't put her off it, maybe it's for real this time."

Even if Barry hadn't been so good to her, often fixing minor things on her truck for free, she wouldn't have declined. His great-great-granddaughter seemed to be a sweet kid. A human sophomore cheerleader who got excellent grades and helped balance Barry's shop books. But, the way MayLee worked with her horse led Carrie to think the teen might stick with being a vet. Carrie suspected MayLee might be an animal empath, just like her.

"It's going to be hot on Thursday. Like one-ten." Even if MayLee got all squirmy on her and bolted, it'd be okay. Carrie usually worked alone anyway.

The huge grin revealed teeth stained by decades of coffee and cigarettes he could no longer have due to a recent heart attack. Who knew gremlins eventually needed to live right or even had hearts? "I'll donate a cooler with cold waters. You need a pop-up canopy and some chairs?"

They hashed out additional details, including getting Barry's fourth wife, the town's secretary, to advertise the clinic on their official website.

Carrie walked back to her truck, if not feeling moderately better about having to shell out the money to get the A/C fixed, at least she could help people. *And* write it off on her taxes. Maybe not really altruistic. She opened her truck's door and stepped back to let Max load up.

A wave of hatred buffeted her and she staggered back, clutching at the truck's door for balance. Her heart stuttered and she shrank back from the stuff of her nightmares, a fury so strong all of the hairs on her body stood on end.

Where?

She spun to put her back to the truck and she fumbled for her knife stashed in her back pocket. Silver. She needed the sacred metal. Her thumb flicked the blade out while her eyes frantically searched the building's shadows. Nothing.

Max's guttural growl and focus pointed her to a shed next to Barry's garage.

No, she wouldn't be that scared girl again. Carrie swallowed hard and pulled hard on her abilities. Like a range-finder, her senses narrowed on the emotional beam targeting her. She gasped.

It couldn't be him. They'd promised he'd never come back. She'd witnessed it.

Witnessed it in all its horror.

Her pulse thundered in her ears, heavier than a cattle stampede. So heavy she almost missed Max's happy yelp. The fury assaulting her morphed to fear, then fled.

She leaned back against her truck, massaging her chest, willing her heart to slow.

Then from the corner of her vision, tactical boots appeared. She lifted her gaze up the long, glorious form of the man leaning his shoulder against her trailer. Her heart started galloping again and air suddenly thinned.

Nathan.

"Carrie." His deep voice rumbled through her, settling low

in her stomach. Max danced at his feet, eager for his attention. Whined in happiness when he reached down to ruffle her ears.

*Little traitor.* Carrie feasted her eyes on his black-clad form, all lean muscle and hardness. The arms crossed at his chest would make any living woman drool. Most of the dead ones too.

She lifted her gaze to his. The cold, gray orbs of a predator practically glowed under a thick mane of blond hair. If anyone personified the alpha wolf, it'd be Nathan Hebert.

"Nathan." It'd come out huskier than she'd wanted. She cleared her throat as she collapsed her knife, then shoved the blade in her back pocket. "What brings you back to Split?" Obviously not her. He'd made it abundantly clear when he'd left three years ago.

He remained silent.

Had her fear ginned up his specter?

"Business."

She'd prepared herself for the answer, but the dart to her heart still stung. "Ah. Well then." Her words stumbled to a halt. *You dumb girl. Where's your pride?* "Hope you find what you're after. Come on, Max."

The dog bounded into the cab and Carrie put her foot on the running board to climb into her pickup.

"Why'd you have your knife out?" He'd been a witness, too. Silent witness to the tribunal's final decision. The golden eyes that blazed hate for all humans had been snuffed out forever.

Her earlier fear could only have been an echo of the past, her senses picking up on something else, amplified by the heat and stress of the day. To think otherwise was crazy, right? "Nothing. Thought I felt something."

If she hadn't known him well, she might've missed the tensing of his shoulders under the black t-shirt. "Enough to bring out your knife? It wasn't nothing. Max seemed to think it was coming from the shed."

"Probably only an animal." She shrugged. "No big deal."

He straightened and started toward the squat shed twenty yards to the side of Barry's shop.

Dammit. She slammed the door shut, told Max to stay. Nathan's broad back filled her view as she trailed behind him. It's not like he'd need backup. As one of the most in-demand private enforcers in the shifter world, she'd be more of a liability to him in a fight. Yet, she followed him to the small structure, if only to prove to him—prove to *herself*—it was nothing.

He stopped about ten feet from the door. The muscles in his back flexed as he took an audible breath. She stepped beside him. His nostrils quivered as if his wolf's sensors tasted what he'd inhaled. He turned to her. "Get in your truck."

The low, grim words sent dread spiraling through her. No. She wouldn't be a victim again. She didn't answer him. Instead, she widened her stance, bent at the knees a bit like her krav maga instructor taught her. That's why she carried her Were knife and carried a smaller version of the sorcerer-spelled silver blade hanging at her neck. With her left hand, she slid the heavy knife from her back pocket and flipped it open.

His jaw hardened and he growled something she couldn't quite catch, but the tone said it all. And while she couldn't sense human emotion, she'd often been able to interpret shifters', since they were bound to their animal. He didn't want her here.

It firmed her resolve. "If you listen closely, you can hear me not caring."

Was it humor or frustration she sensed? Didn't matter. She wouldn't budge.

After several heartbeats, he pointed at her, then to the wall next to the door. He moved to the side with the knob, flattened himself against the wall. The monstrous gun he pulled from his waistband made her large knife look like a butter spreader. The old adage, *You don't bring a knife to a gunfight,* echoed through her mind.

With a three-two-one finger count he reached and turned the knob, flung the door open and curled around the jamb in one fluid motion. Nothing came out snarling or swinging and she let out a shaky breath.

Then the stench hit her. Rotting flesh days gone. She clapped her hand over her mouth, forcing the bile back down to a stomach unwilling to keep it. *Be a professional, girl. You've smelled worse.* "Must've had a dog or cat die in there," she whispered.

The tension pouring off of him didn't make her words feel any more true.

He rolled around the doorframe and into the darkness.

So now it was nut up or shut up. Pride had its drawbacks. She flexed her fingers around the knife, pulled up a shred of courage from somewhere, and tried to approximate the cool motions Nathan executed, plunging herself into the building.

She ran into something solid and fell backward. The knife flew from her hand. With a shriek, she landed on her butt, panic surging through her veins.

A shadow loomed over her.

Garrett. He'd come back from the dead and found her. She scrabbled for the cross at her neck. Pressed the ends of the horizontal bar to release the blade. She snapped it from her neck and thrust it up at the threat. Her hand was swept aside easily. Oh shit.

"Carrie," Nathan barked. He knelt on one knee. "It's me. Stop."

The wolf-shifter came into focus. "I—I—"She couldn't get the words out through teeth that wouldn't stop chattering. What started as trembling turned to violent shaking. She wrapped her hands around her ribs, around the scars, willed him to understand.

He gathered her in his arms. Surrounded her with his warmth, his security. But his protection couldn't make the glowing gold eyes go away completely. Not when the slashes still burned on her ribs. When the bright teeth dripping her own blood had been burned into her memory. "No." She shoved Nathan away and scrambled to her feet. "No. He's dead. I saw it. You saw it. He's not real. Not anymore."

Nathan stepped to the side. In front of them, carnage. The air left her lungs and no matter how hard she pulled, none would enter. Then it did and she couldn't get enough and it sawed through her mouth. Black spots blossomed in her vision, obscuring the mangled body parts bloated with putrefaction.

"No, Carrie." His words came from very far away. "It appears he's very much back."

Blood. Dried blood wrote the words on the far wall.

*Your next Carrie.*

Everything went black.

# CHAPTER 2

Nathan caught Carrie as she crumpled, then scooped her into his arms. He bore her weight with ease. If anything, she'd gotten lighter than three years ago. His wolf's ears picked up the strong beat of her heart, her even breathing. Several strides took him to the garage bay.

"Can I borrow your office?"

A short man who could only be Barry Montez hustled his bulk forward, jaw slackened. "What happened?"

"Problem in your shed." He followed the mechanic and levered her body through the door, while Barry swept papers off an ancient pleather couch.

Nathan placed her on the sagging cushions and stepped back. Drank in her beauty. Her lush pink lips. The freckles bridging her nose. The thick fringe of her eyelashes on the edge of her cheek. He reached forward to tuck back a strand of silky dark copper hair which had escaped her ponytail, then pulled back. He didn't deserve to touch her like that.

Failure weighed on his shoulders. Garrett Frazier—or whoever this was—should be dead. Nathan had witnessed the same ritual as Carrie. After all the clans' placed their protections on the corpse, Frazier shouldn't be running rampant through both the human and paranormal worlds.

The phone in the back pocket of his jeans vibrated. He stepped outside the office and shut the door with a quiet snick, then pulled out his mobile phone and jabbed the green button. "Yes."

"Did you find her?" Sai Baagh's gravelly voice came over the line.

He shoved his free hand through his hair. "Yeah. It's bad. How far out are you?"

Baagh huffed a laugh. "Good ears. I'm pulling into the Split limits. Be there in five or less." The phone beeped indicting the call ended.

Barry stepped in from the bay, wiping his hands on a shop towel. "What happened? Is she okay?"

"She fainted. She'll be fine." He surveyed the gremlin in front of him, whose picture matched his profile. According to Cheese, Nathan's info whiz manning the comms back in the swamp, Barry Montez had a good reputation in the community. A family man, Cheese said. No record with the human police or Council Security. To be sure, Nathan opened his senses. No whiff of fear, just worry. Good enough for now. "Nathan Hebert. Good to finally meet you, Barry." He stuck his hand out.

Barry's face nearly split in two with his smile. A toothy gremlin's grin for sure. He jammed his palm into Nathan's, pumped it heartily. "Good to finally meet you, too, sir. Have you been getting my reports?"

"Absolutely. You've been doing a good job on those repairs for Carrie. Are you sure you don't want compensation?"

"No, no." Barry waved a hand. "She's a good girl. And she needs a break." Gremlin merchants had a propensity to overcharge for services, an extension of their intrinsic bent toward greediness. That he would go without recompense said a lot about his respect for Carrie.

Time for a tougher subject. Nathan crossed his arms, leveled a wolf's glare, the one known far and wide in the paranormal community. Sometimes a reputation was a good thing. "You seem to have a problem with your shed. Anyone or anything been hanging around it lately?"

Barry rearranged his ball cap on his head. "My shed? Nothing." His brows screwed together. "Wait. I saw a big coyote sniffing around there two days ago. Chased it off and haven't seen it since."

"What did it look like?" Nathan held his breath, hoping the answer would be different.

"Big." The hand holding his cap stopped at his shoulder height, right around Nathan's abdomen. "Like twice the size of a regular coyote, more wolf. Black mask and black tail...oh no."

Garrett Frazier's shifted form matched the described color of coyote exactly, as well-known to the paranormal public. Unusual, but not an unknown coloration. Regardless, it made the connection stronger and probable.

Nathan swore under his breath. He'd hoped he'd been wrong, hoped they were only chasing a copycat. "Someone was nailed to the wall in your shed. My estimate, in one hundred-degrees, eighteen to twenty-four hours ago." Nathan's teeth ground at the slick coyote's ability to slip the noose. Frazier killed innocents in Pittsburgh, then arrived in Split to terrorize a woman he tried to kill three years ago.

Barry's chin wobbled. "We see shifters around here all the time. I-I didn't make the connection." His features firmed. "He's dead. That's what I read in the *Enchanted Rock Paranormal Times*. Vampires drained him. Fae cut his head off with the

Sword of Fallen Souls. Human paras burned him. Shifters buried him in a secret grave. Then mages wiped away all traces of him and witches cursed his ashes should his followers want to find them and try to resurrect him." Dark, beady eyes looked up at Nathan for confirmation that the serial killer of the Human Paranormal Clan, HP for short, had truly been eliminated.

"That's what I'd been told." Not exactly true. He and Carrie had been the ceremonial witnesses to the North American Council's judgement. Barry's recitation of events was mostly true, but couldn't match the reality. The feral hatred boiling in Frazier, the foul profanities spewing from the twisted canine's mouth still echoed in his head. The moment he broke free and lunged at Carrie played on endless loop in Nathan's nightmares.

He gazed at the woman he still loved, a slim beam through the metal blinds turning her lashes to sparkling copper. If only in the dream world he could see her like this. Instead, in his nightmares, Frazier reached her and ripped her to shreds while Nathan did nothing but watch in frozen, dickless horror. *Had her scars faded yet? Dammit. You don't deserve to know.*

Sai Baagh's black pickup roared into the parking lot saving Nathan from further comment. "Excuse me. Clan business."

"Of course. I was going to shut my shop. Do you need me for anything?"

"No. Unless you want to stay. This is fixin' to be crawlin' with Shifter Clan Security. Maybe Council Security."

Barry's shoulders twitched and he rolled the edge of his ball cap through his fingers. Gremlins avoided law enforcement of any kind like they had rabies. "Uh, no. Lock up when y'all are done?"

"You bet." The fewer bystanders they had to this shitshow,

the better. "And Barry, keep this on the D-L. No one, not even your wife, knows about Frazier."

The mechanic nodded, then hurried away in time to avoid Baagh.

Nathan suppressed a chuckle. The large weretiger made many people nervous. With reason. Taller by several inches than Nathan, with almost as much cunning, most beings wilted when pinned with his green-gold gaze. Nathan's alpha wolf refused to bend and met Baagh with a direct look and outstretched hand.

"Brother Hebert." Baagh used the Cajun 'A-bear' pronunciation of Nathan's last name, then clasped Nathan's forearm below the elbow in the ancient shifter warrior greeting. Pleasantries over, he got down to business. "Situation?"

"Dismembered body in the shed." He hooked a thumb toward the building. "Unknown decedent, but by the smell, I suspect an HP. Looks like he was killed elsewhere and dumped here. Words written in blood indicating Carrie's next. Thought I got a whiff of Frazier, but the decay's too rank. My tracker's inbound with the rest of the team, but if you have one handy, you could get an earlier confirmation."

"I'll wait for yours, since she's already got the stench from that piece of shit in her nose." Baagh planted his massive hands on his hips and swore a long, creative string. "We can't keep a lid on this forever. Soon we're going to have to bring in NAC Security. If the HP find out Frazier is back and murdering their own and we didn't tell them? And if all the other Pure Paranormal advocates find out, this will embolden them. It'll make the Rome massacre look like my niece's first birthday party."

"Didn't you tell me your brother and sister-in-law's families went at it and twenty shifters ended up in the med ward?"

He cocked an eyebrow. "Yep."

"Right." 'Brother' or not, angering a tiger meant taking your life in your own hands. "What's next? I don't think he's going to give up on killin' her. You've confirmed he was involved in Minister Benneman's assassination last year?"

The weretiger nodded with a jerk of his chin. "DNA from Council archives confirmed it."

Yet another reason to get to Frazier before the HP found out their Minister to the NAC had been assassinated by a supposed dead werecoyote.

Assuming it was Frazier?

*Whoa.*

It had to be him. Right? Everything pointed to it. Victim profile, eyewitness accounts, the two hairs recovered at Benneman's murder scene, scooped up surreptitiously by Baagh himself. Nathan eyed the weretiger. No. He had no reason to believe Baagh was dirty. Frazier did this, alright.

But something smelled off. And he'd learned to trust his instincts in all things. The last time he hadn't, it almost cost Carrie her life.

Nathan couldn't soften the additional bad news. "I think he took out the security personnel involved in puttin' him down. I had Cheese trying to locate them, but all five have gone missing."

"Even Tuloq?" The tiger's voice dropped to a bare rumble. The polar bear had been the prior Clan Shifter security chief and Baagh's mentor.

It was Nathan's turn to nod. Tuloq's family were currently on a desperate hunt for the werebear.

The Chief's hands balled into fists. "Carrie's our one lead in this," he snarled. "He wants her."

The implication jabbed Nathan's heart. "No."

He'd been planning to take her away until the threat ended.

Not use her as bait. He'd almost lost her once through his own stupidity, he couldn't gamble she'd lose her life to this rabid dog.

"He'll be going after Council members next. If he gets to them, it'll throw everything into chaos and Clan Shifter will be blamed. We have to find who resurrected him. We can't let shifters take the fall for this. Carrie will understand her duty to the NAC." Baagh narrowed his green-gold eyes. "I called you in because you're the best security contractor in the paranormal world. And I was hoping she'd still listen to you. Am I wrong?"

In many things, no. In this? Carrie would not understand. He needed to take the tiger down a peg. "You called me in because my team's the best and you don't want NAC Security to know about it."

For a moment, it appeared the other shifter would take exception, then his face turned crafty. "I knew I could count on you to see it my way. My whole team can back you up."

Nathan shook his head. "If you do that, it leaves clan leadership vulnerable. What if this is only a diversion?" His strength was contingency planning and strategy. It kicked into full effect. "I'll take five of your best."

"If you think that's all it'll take, I've got five in mind. All wolves."

"I'll take 'em." If Baagh trusted them, he would too. They'd think like him, they'd move like him, they'd hunt like him.

Behind them, the office door opened and both shifters turned.

Carrie stalked out, head held high. "I'm going home." She pivoted and started toward her truck. The throng of shifters in the parking lot which had gathered during Nathan and the weretiger's discussion swayed and parted like marsh grass in a strong wind.

"Carrie, stop," Baagh commanded.

Unlike shifters, humans didn't have to obey a higher pack animal. Nathan started after her.

He placed his hand on her arm as she grasped the door handle to her truck. "Carrie—"

A Fury whirled on him, knocking his hand away and sweeping his feet from under him.

It'd been a long time since someone got the drop on him. He'd forgotten the pavement's hardness, and how much it hurt when his skull bounced off it. His head spun.

She reached for something in her back pocket.

Thankfully, he still had her knife. Otherwise, she might've plunged it into his heart. A fatal blow with a spelled silver blade would be a hard one to overcome, even given his reputation.

Her features cleared, then her brow creased. Perfect lips formed an 'O'. She backed up, calves bumping into her truck's running boards.

And the babble of voices around them? Silence. Probably everyone as shocked as he at the shifter legend's takedown by lowly HP Carrie Fletcher. Where had she found those skills? Hadn't she fainted not ten minutes ago?

She shooed Max to the other side, clambered into her still-idling truck and put it in gear.

Shit. He leapt to his feet, ran after the truck until he reached the cab. He jumped, landed on the running boards and put a hand on her shoulder.

She thrust her left palm, leading with the heel. Something crunched when it connected.

A haze of agony flooded in his face. He lost his grip and fell off the truck. A roll brought him to a crouch.

She gunned it. Didn't even slow at the stop sign for Main

Street. The truck roared around the corner, trailer swaying crazily.

Had she looked for traffic? He swiped at the trickle sensation under his nose and came away with a bloody streak on his hand. Dammit. He sprinted into the garage.

Baagh stood at the bay opening and handed him a paper shop towel with a smirk. "Never thought I'd see you bested by a HP. Maybe I need to think about calling in another bad-ass, 'cause you just got yours handed to you, son."

He grabbed the towel from the tiger's hand and tore two hunks from it. "She's been workin' with Alannah's personal security trainer." His words sounded nasal. They should since she'd crushed his nose. He wadded the paper into rolls and jammed them up his nostrils, suppressing a wince. He'd heal soon enough. "Have your team meet at Carrie's. Cheese's back in the bayou running logistics and intel. I've got Suds with me picking up supplies. The other three are due in tonight."

The tiger shifter shot him the side eye. "Fuzzy, too?"

"You shouldn't hold Indianapolis against him. It's been over a year now." He'd kept his face serious, but a trace of humor crept in to his tone and the shifters snickered. Then the urgency plowed its way back to the top priority. Carrie had turned toward home, but no one protected her. If it *was* Garrett, he'd know where to find her, even if she'd kept the witch-warded shield on her property. The crafty coyote would find a way through.

He rubbed the back of his skull where it had impacted the pavement. Carrie may have upped her self-defense game.

But that alone wouldn't save her from a rabid *rougarou* bent on revenge.

# CHAPTER 3

Carrie made it home by sheer will. Once she put the truck in park, all her energy slipped away. She folded her arms on the steering wheel and rested her forehead on them. Max licked her ear, and she turned, burying her face in comfort of her dog's soft fur.

It had been two years since her last panic attack. She'd thought her blades and self-defense classes would keep her from being a victim again. A self-deprecating laugh slipped from her lips. *Fool. You should've known Garrett would live up to his last words. Even if he has horrible grammar.*

The tiny humor about the bloody words lifted her spirits, enough to pull herself away from her pup and try to find her center. No doubt Nathan would be hot on her heels.

She settled back, closed her eyes and concentrated on locating her calm. All thoughts entered a bucket which tipped to pour out when full enough, refilling at a slower pace, emptying again, until nothing remained to fill it and her heart-beat and breathing came back to normal. Finally, she returned to reality. Ten minutes had passed.

Time to move. She clambered from the cab, legs wobbling far more than she'd like. A deep breath in, then she plowed forward, while Max ranged into the grass. A few steps later, Carrie reached the trailer. The soothing balm of the mindless work of restocking her supplies called to her.

Three hundred yards distant, a black SUV emerged through the witch-warded illusion field at the end of her driveway and sped toward her.

Dammit. She hadn't asked her cousin Helena to take Nathan out of the people permitted to see her driveway, thirty acres of land, house, and barn. Dark-tinted windows and Louisiana plates said it was one of Hebert Security's own vehicles. Nathan's blond head glowed gold in the front passenger seat.

Her fragile calm couldn't take it, so she entered the trailer where her OCD about locking everything down continued to pay off. Nothing seemed out of place after the wild ride from Barry's garage. She flipped on the electricity which engaged the A/C unit, then pulled open the first drawer, marked 'GLOVES: Standard Exam; OB Sleeves'. Two and a half boxes of standard exam gloves. Not yet at her restock threshold. She moved to the next holdout. Geez. How many of the shoulder-length gloves had she blown through during the pregnancy checks at Cal Brown's cattle operation?

The side door she'd used opened, flooding the interior with sunlight, stirring the dim, still stifling interior. "Carrie."

For a moment she didn't recognize Nathan's voice with its nasal inflection. She flipped her gaze over her shoulder and spied his blond mane. Yep. She went back to her routine. Twelve? She'd used twelve sleeves? She noted the number. Oh yeah, Bonnie McLaren's cow had the difficult birth this morning, and she'd torn holes in a couple of them using the calf puller. She scribbled at the bottom of the sheet pinned to her clipboard, 'Need new chain connectors to the calf-puller'. She shut the drawer and moved to the next down marked 'SPONGES: Gauze, Drain, Foam'.

"Carrie. We need to talk."

"No. We don't." She paused counting the boxes of paper-wrapped gauze sponges. She'd used a load of them that morning on Tom Hawley's dog that had gotten in a fight with what could only have been a coyote. "Go away."

"Please come out. I need to talk to you."

His patient words inexplicably made her angrier. "Go. Away."

"There's not a lot of room in there. I don't want you freakin' out when I come in." His tone mimicked the same soothing croon she'd use with an injured animal.

At five-ten, Carrie could stand upright without her head hitting the metal. Nathan would be cramped at six-foot-four, almost worth the humor, but not the close quarters with him. She huffed and slammed the cabinet door shut, dropped the aluminum clipboard on the stainless-steel counter with a clatter. "Fine."

She barreled down the two short stairs, fast enough Nathan stepped back. Good. Someone needed to be afraid of her. She flipped the trailer's generator off, slammed the trailer's door, then stomped off toward her single-story ranch house. If they had to have this discussion, they could at least do it with a cold glass of tea. She didn't even turn to see if he followed her. Once through the door, she left it open then shed her muck-covered boots and set them in their plastic holding pan.

The click of the latch said he'd entered her house. Something she thought she'd never live to witness again, no matter how she'd once longed for it. He'd be gone soon enough, right? If she could keep her defenses up...

"Boots," she said. As thumps echoed on the Saltillo tile, she stalked to the cabinet in her sock feet. She pulled two glasses, filled them with ice, then again with cold tea from a vat in her refrigerator. Beads of sweat slid down her back. She placed one glass on the counter and tipped the other to her lips. The cool beverage slid down her throat, and she sighed in pleasure. Socked footfalls brought her hackles back up. She shoved her hands on her hips, gritted her teeth and lifted her gaze to her former lover.

Two bits of blue shop towel plugged his nose, each streaked with dark red blood. Both eyes sported blue-black crescents under them and his whole nasal bridge was swollen to twice its size.

She gasped. "I did that to you?" Her resolve hardened against traitorous sympathies. Shifters healed at a ridiculous rate. He'd be fine in the morning, if not later this evening. If he hadn't put his hands on her, he wouldn't have blue shop towel bits hanging from his nose.

He pulled the plugs from his nostrils and wadded them in his palms. "I shouldn't have put my hands on you."

She spewed out the tea, then mopped at it with a sponge. Since when did Nathan start reading minds, let alone express regret for something? "Yeah, well, apology accepted." She stopped obsessively cleaning and placed the sponge exactly one inch on the top and left side on the sink's deck. Readjusted it to her satisfaction. "So, say what you have to say, then get out."

"That's the problem. I'm not leavin'. Not until we catch Frazier." His stance, legs wide and leaning forward, signaled he wouldn't back down. "Baagh hired me to guard you."

"I don't care what Sai Baagh said or hired you to do. Shifter isn't my clan. And you're not staying here." She glared at him.

"I know how you feel—"

"Really? *You* know how *I* feel?" She rushed around the island as his years-old betrayal hit her hot and hard, blowing through any panic she might've felt earlier. "You *pretend* to know how I feel?" She stabbed her finger almost on his broken nose, then pulled up. Too revealing. She stepped back several paces.

"I know I hurt you when I left, but—"

*Divert.* "That's what you think this is about?" she sneered. "You and me were over three years ago. Three *years*." She didn't let him answer. "This is about Garrett Frazier. The male who murdered my parents. You promised—hell, the entire freaking Council promised—he couldn't come back. Yet somehow, he has."

"Yes. It appears he has." His shoulders bunched.

"Appears?"

Nathan rubbed the back of his neck. "I don't know. It doesn't feel right."

"Feel right?" she echoed. "It sure felt like him—" Shoot. Too much.

His icy gaze narrowed on her. "It felt like him?"

"Seemed like him." Maybe he'd accept the correction. She shrugged and picked up her tea. Sipped the cold brew. Couldn't stand the weight of his scrutiny anymore and blurted, "I felt rage. It was the same fury, Garrett's same wavelength. Then you showed up and the emotion turned to fear. Then he disappeared." She put her tea down before her shaking hands spilled it.

"I know you don't want me here, but I'm not gonna leave you to face this alone." He spread his hands wide. "The team is due around midnight tonight. I've only got Suds with me. Damn coyote moved faster than I expected."

"What? You knew about this and didn't tell me? How long has he been back?" Her words ended on a shriek. How did she not know?

In a fluid move he crossed to her, concern coloring his features. "We didn't want to alarm you. I know how hard you worked to try to gain some normalcy."

She put her hands on his chest and pushed him away, a physical manifestation of what he did three years ago. "How would you know? You left me."

His face shuttered. "I kept up with Alannah. Made sure Lisa Manu kept an eye on you as well."

She swung away and propped her hands on the counter. The leader of the Human Paranormals, Alannah, HP Clan representative to the NAC, and current Minister had been exceptionally nice to her. Calling periodically. Making sure to hook Carrie up with Alannah's own self-defense teacher. Someone she'd come to call a friend. But the NAC Minister hadn't given her the time of day until Nathan left.

Then Lisa Manu, the ocelot who currently headed Clan Shifter. Carrie had become veterinarian to the shifters, treating a shifter when it was too injured to change. But they'd had their own vets within the clan, and even the subclans.

Until Nathan left.

All of this didn't happen until Nathan left her. That he'd manipulated her like a simple piece of origami paper burned. As if she could be bought off after their affair. Her gullibility, the ease at which she'd been seduced, then tossed away, flamed again and seared her like a branding iron.

Nathan stepped behind her, the natural shifter's heat

adding to the blaze of her fury, her humiliation, until it became a blast furnace, ready to ignite the entire universe.

She whirled to face him. "Leave me the hell alone. I don't need *you*. I don't need your meddling. Garrett died. This is someone's sick joke." She jabbed her index finger into his chest. *Ow.* His chest was like granite, but if she could make it hurt all the way to his heart, it would be but an infinitesimal fraction of the pain he'd caused her. She added her best snarl to her words and doubled up on the force of her finger, "Get out of my house."

For several moments she glared up at him. Then she realized where she'd worked herself. Into the crook of the counter, with his glorious body nearly touching hers. His heat. His smell. Pine and citrus and all male.

Her knees wavered. *Oh no.*

She pushed at his abdomen. "Back up." She repressed a wince at the breathy whisper. If he knew how much she still longed for him, what they still shared in her dreams, it'd be more humiliating than when she found out about his fiancée. "And get out." Better.

He stepped back three paces, his eyes hard, icy chips. "Killin' an HP isn't a 'sick joke'. And it's nice you think I'm gonna leave because you want me to, *chere*. Frazier's back. I've been hired to capture him."

The French endearment in his sinful Cajun drawl caused familiar flutters in her belly. He had to go. "You were there as an official witness at his destruction with me. How did he come back?" She laid the disbelief on thick.

"It's not my job to figure out *how* he came back. It's my job to capture him." He leaned toward her, palms on the counter. "Again."

"And how are you going to trap him?"

He lifted a brow and smiled apologetically.

Her stomach twisted. "No. Oh no. No. You are not using me as bait for some freak Garrett Frazier wannabe.'

A muscle ticked in his cheek. "He's coming for you anyway, *chere*."

She swallowed hard, willing the shivers his words brought to still. "Fine. Then let's call Council Security. They can watch over me. Like you did back then." *Low blow*.

He took two steps forward, crowded her back into the corner again. "*They* called *me*." His words emerged from clenched teeth. "Only I've been able to catch him. You know what happened to the others who tried."

The weight of inevitability crushed her. "Can't someone else—"

"No. He's already here." He swung away, shoved his fingers through his hair, ruffling the thick strands, then pivoted back to face her. "You don't get it. The show in Barry's shed was meant to terrify you, and you don't even have the sense to be scared."

She had zero sense. Maybe even negative sense. Because she still loved Nathan Hebert.

And that scared her more than Garrett Frazier ever could.

# CHAPTER 4

Nathan's stomach rumbled and he slammed the refrigerator door shut. "You have nothin' to eat."

"There's plenty in there. Excuse me if I wasn't expecting to have to feed a pack of carnivores," Carrie said, tone as sweet as a ton of cane sugar. From her position curled up on the couch, she motioned toward the oversized bowl she held with her other hand. "I can make you another salad of mixed greens with kale and spinach, pumpkin seeds, blueberries. Some yummy quinoa." She waved her fork loaded with some sort of tiny round grain and leaves at him with an evil smile before popping it in her mouth.

Ugh. Even Max couldn't bring herself to beg for a bite and had stretched out on her dog bed in the corner.

His genius was for tactical thinking. Why hadn't he taken her vegetarian status into consideration during planning? Because Frazier moved too quickly. He and the team had him cornered in Pittsburgh, where the evil coyote targeted a leading shifter and HP supporter, along with her family. Two prominent bear shifters and four cubs active in clan politics dead. He would never be able to unsee the desecration to the bodies, the scrawled profanities and slogans in the victims' blood. He shoved those visions into a box and put a lid on them, choosing instead to dwell on how Frazier got past the security and its implications—the *rougarou* possibly had help from the fae, Magic, Shifter, or Sanguis Clans.

Worse, Cheese had worked on a hunch, pulling death reports targeting murders of shifters known to support Human Paranormals. He found enough hints sprinkled throughout North America that the clan couldn't keep it from their general population for long, enough that there had to be similar numbers in the other clans. Why the Pure Paranormal crowd wouldn't be shouting Frazier's return from the hills he couldn't understand. Unless their unmasking last time drove them to believe they needed to work within the shadows. Could sympathizers in other clans be actively hiding the activities?

He shook his head, as if the action would erase the questions demanding answers. It didn't matter why right now. Nathan had to bring Frazier in before wider panic within shifters spread to the whole paranormal world and the *rougarou*'s toxic message gained more strength. Thus far, Clan Shifter's leadership managed to stifle it within their community.

From worse to pure shit sandwich was Nathan and Cheese suspected the murders weren't only within the shifter world. It meant hacking into the other clans' security systems. Contrary to popular movie lore, hacks took time. Something Nathan had little of at the moment.

He wished the sick feeling Frazier played him would go away. Instead, the coyote led him like a *fifolet* in an unfamiliar, dangerous swamp—if he followed the light, he'd be lost for sure. But how could he not when the malevolent coyote threatened Carrie?

The loud grumble of his stomach brought him back to his lack of meat. At least he'd been able to pull the shop towels out. By the dull pain, the delicate nasal bones knitted. It should be right in the morning.

Unlike his current situation.

If he were true with himself, he'd admit his poor planning had nothing to do with Frazier and everything to do with seeing Carrie again. He'd kept up vicariously through everyone in her life—from Barry to neighbors on all four sides of her. Even Alannah. After he failed to keep her safe from the coyote, it had been obvious Carrie would need an army.

His gaze settled on the woman he'd forced himself to love from afar. His wolf howled inside for his mate. She'd barely changed. Same long, slim form, a little more slender than when he left. She wore her hair longer by at least a foot. His fingers itched to thread their way through the silky strands. His wolf snarled, paced, demanded he claim her. If only he could.

Her lashes lifted and their gazes tangled.

He hated his responsibility for the wary glint in her gorgeous brown eyes. For a heartbeat, the apology hovered on the edge of his tongue.

Carrie rose from the couch, brushed by him, and washed her bowl and fork, setting them in the drainboard. She started toward the back door on the opposite side of the kitchen.

"Where are you heading?" His words emerged as a bark.

"The barn. The animals have a feeding schedule." She jammed her socked feet into worn boots sitting in a low-lipped pan identical to the one at her front door. When she bent over to adjust the hems of her jeans, his mouth watered. Morning showers often heavily involved fantasies about that ass.

Before he could recover, she'd bolted out the door, swinging it shut behind her with a bang. "Wait." He raced for his tactical boots still at the front door, jammed them on, and zipped up the sides.

Even if Baagh's crew had been briefed and were out on patrol, he couldn't leave her unprotected.

Nathan caught her before she went into the barn, which sat a hundred yards from the house. "Carrie, wait." The team searched the outbuildings, but her security hung on his shoulders, a heavy burden.

Mercifully, she halted and Nathan gave silent thanks. He took this job to protect her, not fight her. He pulled his forty-five auto from the holster inside the back of his waistband. The sorcerer-spelled silver bullets would at least slow the monster down if Nathan couldn't penetrate anything important.

The barn's doors remained open after his team of six searched it. He wanted as much light and as many sight lines as possible. Plus, if he had to make entry, those damn sliding doors squealed more than *Maman* Rae's pet sow and would announce his arrival.

He removed his phone from his back jean's pocket and stabbed his finger on the radio app icon connecting all of the team. "Check in."

One by one, the six checked in.

"Ten-four. At barn." S-O-P would've been to check in before they left the house to make sure their perimeter hadn't been compromised and all were available to respond if necessary. He slid a glance to Carrie, who waited for him with barely concealed impatience, arms crossed, booted toe tapping. They'd already fought enough for now. He'd save that battle for later tonight. "Stay behind me."

An eye roll worthy of his fourteen-year old niece was his only answer.

He moved forward, burst through the door, gaze darting to every corner. Something rushed his knees and butted him. He tried to regroup, but a blow from the other side pushed him backward and down. Then he got a big load of goo right in the eyes. Dammit. He wiped his left forearm over his face, trying to erase the slime. He needed to see the threat. Then Carrie's smothered laughter and Max's barks hit his ears.

Finally, his vision cleared and he observed his attackers.

A goat, a donkey, and a llama. What the hell? His gaze skidded around the barn. Not simply those, but a host of animals. Sheep. Chickens. A horse. Several more donkeys. Two rabbits. A peacock. More goats. All focused on him. All emitting a distinctly unfriendly vibe. Except for Max, who stood between him and the angry mob, hackles raised.

"I don't think they like you." Carrie choked out the words over her giggles. "Billy Bumps, Rusty, Stinky back off." She waved her hand back. "Max, lie."

Magically, the beasts obeyed. Yet dark, baleful eyes tracked him as he rose from the concrete. The shifter security legend, rolled twice in one day. First by a civilian, then by a herd of animals. He stuffed his gun in its holster. Thank the Gods he didn't shoot one of them. At least he didn't have an audience this time, unless you counted the beasts.

"Okay, folks. Listen up." Carrie's voice held a stern tone.

The rooting, clucking, braying and snuffling silenced.

Fists jammed on her hips, she surveyed the crowd. A small furrow developed between her brows. "This is Nathan." She hooked a thumb to him. "He's cool, okay?"

For a moment nothing happened. The weight of more than twenty pairs of eyes assessing him became unnerving. Did they smell the wolf on him? Then the chickens started pecking, the goats turned to root in the hay. They'd accepted him just like that? One of the sheep moved off and something struck him about its halting gait.

It only had three legs.

The donkey. It had a prosthetic leg. The horse bumped into the stall's jamb on its way back to the little enclosure. When it turned, both eyes were milky. Blind. His mind boggled at these animals' needs.

"Not all of them are."

He found his voice. "Are what?"

"Special needs." The goat which attacked him earlier nudged her leg and she scratched it behind the ears. "Billy Bumps had a bowel obstruction and his owners didn't want to pay for surgery." She pointed at the tripod sheep. "That's Pansy. She got stepped on by her mother and broke her leg as a lamb." Carrie moved further into the barn in the direction of a tack room set in the corner.

For a moment, he considered stopping her, since he hadn't cleared the building yet. The animals halted him. If the *rougarou* hung around, they wouldn't be this relaxed.

She opened the door and started scooping feed into a pail. Carried it to the stall where the horse waited, then dumped it into a larger bucket attached to the wall. She stroked the animal's neck, worked her strong hands down its body, down the legs while it fed.

His gaze focused on the action and his mouth went dry.

"Nosey's owner was going to put him down at birth," she said, yanking him from his nascent fantasies. Apparently satisfied with Nosey's condition, she stood and scratched him under the cheek as the animal chewed. "Shame. He's a good horse."

She received a nicker and a nuzzle in her neck as if he understood her words of praise. "And quite the love bug."

More scoops and more feedings followed, with explanations of each animal and how she'd come to care for them. Most were merely unwanted and she attempted to find them new homes. Then they reached the final stall, where the llama stood in the far corner from the door. He didn't need Carrie's abilities as an animal empath to know this one had a bad attitude. The ugly glare from its big, round eyes said it all.

"And Stinky, here...well..." She quirked a smile. As quick as a snake, Stinky reared and hurled a wad of spit at him.

If not for Nathan's preternatural reflexes, the goo would've hit him in the face again, instead of landing on the concrete with a mushy, moist *whack*.

She smirked. "He still has trust issues with men." As soon as she'd dumped the feed in its dish, Stinky rushed toward her. A practiced sidestep removed her from its path. The llama buried its head in the bucket then came back up to chew. Carrie stroked its neck, scratched the tuft of longer hair between its ears. "Someone found him dumped on their property. From what I can sense, he's been abused. It's taken months to get this far." She murmured with each stroke. And with each stroke, the animal's muscles relaxed.

As did his. Then it hit him. Carrie was more than an empath. She could speak her love to them on an emotional level.

Her soft, shimmering brown gaze met his. "What?"

Shit. He'd been staring. Yet he couldn't seem to look away. "Admirin' your way with animals, *chere*." His belly tightened as his blood began to heat.

Her lashes swept down. "Don't call me that," she said, her

flat tone carrying an arctic chill. She stalked forward and brushed past him as she exited the stall.

He reined in his wolf. *Down boy.* She couldn't have said 'leave me the fuck alone' more clearly. He followed her, her ass really, to the tack room, where she tidied up, dumping more feed into the metal bins, dropping the lids with metallic clangs. She crossed toward him, then tossed a push broom to him.

He caught it out of pure reflex.

"If you're going to stand there, you can at least sweep." Challenge echoed in her words. "Start at the door." She poked her finger the way they'd entered. "Work your way here." She pivoted and disappeared back into the tack room.

*Sweep?* Indignation rose. He was the best security strategist money could buy, not a stable boy.

"Either you do it, or we'll be out here longer while I do it after I'm done in here," she said from the door as she pushed a pile of dirt with her own broom through the room's threshold and into the main area. She stooped and filled a bucket with water from a hose looped on the wall. Mop and sudsy bucket in hand, she disappeared again.

He shook his head and began the repetitive motion. Several minutes later, he pushed the surprisingly large pile of dust, debris and bits of dried animal shit out the far barn door. He wiped his brow. The heat of day had begun to tail off with impending twilight, but August in Central Texas still packed a punch. Not as humid as the bayous of Morgan City, but the extra fifteen degrees more than made up for it. A beer would be good right now. The weight of observation fell on him and he spun to find Carrie leaning on her mop, studying him, a small smile curling the ends of her generous lips.

"What?"

"Didn't think you'd really sweep. Thought you'd believe it below you."

He had. But he wouldn't let her know that. "Felt good to get a little sweat going."

"Uh huh." She hefted the bucket to a sink on the outside wall of the tack room.

He started forward. "Here, let me do that." His hand covered hers over the handle. He almost pulled away. Zings. The little sparks of electricity still arced between them.

She stilled. "I can do it," her voice dipped to a whisper.

For several moments he stared at their connection, breath caught by his yearnings, until she yanked her hand out from under his.

"Thanks. We'll be mucking stalls tomorrow." For all the warmth in her voice, he could've been anyone. He tracked her, hunger growing as she crossed barn, her back stiff as the metal broom handle he still held.

Had he imagined the connection still existed? Or was it only on his side?

Nathan trailed after her. He'd left his mate behind after Frazier's judgement, believing since he hadn't been able to protect her from the *rougarou*, he didn't deserve to have her. Since then, no one else filled his mind, his dreams.

And now his waking fantasies.

# CHAPTER 5

C arrie forced herself to walk rather than run back to the house, forced herself to leave the back door unlocked rather than throwing the bolt, forced herself to quell the desire for him she'd believed long conquered.

She snagged two beers from the refrigerator and pulled the caps off. She set one on the counter for him, wandered to the couch. If she couldn't remain calm around Nathan, she'd be right back where she'd been three years ago. Sobbing, curled into a ball in her bed. He'd left her before, he'd leave her again. Right?

*Right.*

But the minute he'd come into view, all sleek, lean, golden wolf, what they'd shared came rolling back in a tsunami of craving for his touch, his quick, dark humor.

*Gah.* She was so screwed. A long pull on the cold beer cooled her body down a bit, but couldn't put out the fires Nathan's proximity stoked.

The back door closed with a quiet snick. She kept her gaze trained out the bay window. The Western face of Enchanted

Rock rose some five miles distant. The sunset highlighted the rusty dome's color, making it glow almost neon to those who could see the vortex's energy signature.

"Your father picked a great spot for a front-row seat." He gestured with his beer bottle, then sat in a large, brown club chair, the same one her dad used to sit in and stare out at the dome of rock after particularly difficult council meetings.

"Umm." She took a sip from her bottle after the non-committal sound. Had Dad ever regretted his involvement in politics? If he hadn't been the HP Councilman during Garrett Frazier's Pure Paranormal reign of terror, would he and Mom still be alive?

Max popped through the doggie door and padded to lay at Nathan's feet on the cool tile.

The small betrayal tipped the scale. The day's stress and frustration bubbled over. She needed a shower and sleep, in that order. "Sheets are already on the beds in the spare rooms and the bathrooms have towels." She drained her beer and rose. "I've got appointments starting at seven. Need to leave by six-thirty."

"No."

"No what?" She planted her hands on her hips. "You're not sleeping in my bed."

A muscle worked in his cheek. "No, you're not goin' to your appointments," he said through clenched teeth.

She tried to get the raging fury under control before she said something she really regretted. To buy time, she crossed to the kitchen, tossed her empty bottle into recycling and slammed the lid. Then she took a deep breath and said through stiff lips, "The heck I'm not. I don't know where you get off coming back in here like you have the right to order me around." If she didn't make her appointments, she didn't get paid. She stabbed her finger into the counter. "I've got customers to see. If I don't, I lose them to another vet."

His face had turned to granite. "You can reschedule."

"No. I can't." She bit the words out carefully, as if explaining to a kindergartner. "If you're running a big cattle operation, you aren't rounding up your herd only to have me reschedule last minute."

He appeared to consider for a moment, then crossed his arms. "This is non-negotiable. You're stayin' here, where you're safer."

"You're gonna have to tie me up to keep me here." Two could play at the crossed arms game.

His eyes lit with fire and a corner of his lip curled as if considering the possibilities.

The memory of their last physical encounter floated through her brain unbidden. They had done just that—tying up. Her cheeks burst into flame, causing her to nearly lose her bravado. "Besides, I thought you were the best security Clan Shifter can buy."

"I am."

"Then I'll be fine." She whirled around, headed to her bedroom.

"Carrie."

His tone morphed from hard to coaxing and despite her desire to have the last word, she halted.

"Here we have a plan, a known set of parameters. We can lure him to us. But out in the field, he could be around any corner, waitin' to kill you."

"I get it, but I'm still going." She held a hand up as he made to say more. "The last time Garrett had my family under siege in our own house, but still managed to murder my parents and almost kill me. I'm not living in fear in my own home." The scars on her ribs began to burn in memory as she tried to suppress a violent shudder. She clutched at the amulets and knife around her neck, searching for the Clan Magic charm. Since her mom was a mage, she'd earned the amulet by blood and could enter the Clan's town hidden from the normal world to visit family. The cool gem slid through her fingers. "I swore I'd never live like that again."

He huffed an aggrieved breath. "That's what I'm tryin' to tell you. I failed to protect you once. I can't let it happen again." The tiniest bit of something stark flitted across his face. Pain?

No surely not. She pulled on the reins of her anger and applied her talent. Guilt. Why would he feel guilty? "You hold yourself responsible for that?"

All expression left his features.

"Holy crap. You *do*." *How... Why...* How in the ever-living heck could he feel responsible for another's actions? She pulled her bowl and fork from the drainboard and methodically opened the cupboard. Deposit dish. She opened the drawer. Deposit fork. She pulled it back out and rubbed at a water spot on it with a dishtowel then put it back. Nope, the concept still bounced around without making a connection. She folded the cloth into its neat rectangle and placed it carefully back on the granite. Turned it until it mapped in perfect alignment with the sink.

Finally, she turned to him, considered his form, backlit by the waning twilight. "Since for the life of me I can't figure out how you'd hold yourself responsible for someone else's actions, let alone deny the fact you saved me from being killed by said someone, you're gonna have to explain it to me."

A crack appeared in his stony features. Bit by bit it crumbled until it revealed the raw pain behind the mask. "He shouldn't have been close enough to touch you, let alone kill your parents and—" In an instant, the hard, expressionless exterior returned to his features. "I failed."

"No. You caught *the* Garrett Frazier, serial murderer of HPs and their supporters. Brought him to justice." How could he believe he failed? She threw up her hands. "You saved countless Leftovers from a horrible death. How could you have failed?

"Don't call yourself that." He looked away from her and raked a hand through his hair.

His hard tone caught her unaware. *Leftover.* A pejorative term for HPs. It derived from the residual powers found in the children resulting from the matings of humans to paranormal beings. The HPs themselves widely used the word, mainly as a way to take it back from those like Garret Frazier who thought the HPs didn't deserve immortal status, let alone a seat on the Council.

"Why do you care what I call myself?" she whispered. She caught his gaze, gray irises carrying the bleakness of harsh winter. Her breath hung in her throat. Heartbeats passed and the ice began to melt.

"Because you're not a Leftover," he said. "You're a beautiful person who deserves the dignity of being acknowledged for your unique gifts. Your heart's capacity for love. Your devotion to those most would throw away is inspiring."

She had to look down, unable to bear the intensity in his gaze. "I'm not a beautiful person, not an inspiration." She swiped at the moisture on her cheeks. "I'm a mess. I can barely keep up with my bills. My truck is ancient. I wouldn't even have this ginormous house if it hadn't been my parents'." The last word broke on a sob.

Large, warm arms circled her, engulfing her in the unfamiliar cloak of safety. For a moment she tried to hold back the wave, then the damn broke, and she buried her nose in his shirt and let the tears fall. Tears of pain, tears of loss. Of want. Of...hope.

She stiffened. No. She couldn't let her defenses down. Not after the last time he left. She wedged her hands between them. Pushed away from the only thing she'd ever really wanted for her own. Inexplicably, it made her cry all the harder. She pivoted away, attempting to hide her weakness.

"Carrie..." he murmured.

She could feel the heat of his body behind her, calling her to give in to his strength, tempting her. *No.* A tissue from the counter's box helped her regain some semblance of self-respect. Finally, she could face him. She scraped together as much dignity as possible before she turned. "I'm going to ask Sai to find someone else."

"Why?" His eyes searched hers, as if the answer was to be found there.

"You can't be here because I loved you, Nathan." At the last moment she covered her true feelings by using the past tense. She couldn't bear for him to know it existed very much in the present.

He froze, horror plain in his features.

"Don't worry." She choked a forced laugh. "I just thought I loved you. It was infatuation and gratitude. We'd hardly known each other a couple of weeks, right? Love. As if." She swung away from him. "I'll call Sai Baagh in the morning."

His hand stopped her. Gentle this time. Not like earlier that evening when her instincts kicked in and she'd dropped him out of pure reaction. "Wait," he said.

She didn't dare lift her gaze, her walls approached critical mass, close to being breeched. She couldn't repair them again.

His finger lifted her chin nonetheless. Warm gray eyes met hers. "I ran away, Carrie. I was in love with you and beyond stupid. I thought you couldn't love me after I failed you. I ran, sure you would come to hate me for not protecting you and your parents." His hand rose, tenderly cupped her cheek.

For a moment, all that registered was 'in love with you' and her heart grew to near exploding. Then his remaining words sunk in. Heat exploded in her belly and she slapped his hand away. "You thought you knew what was best for me? You—" she sputtered, her fury choking off word formulation.

"I'm sorry, Carrie. It was stupid." He rubbed the back of his neck. "I was being unreasonable, pushing you away."

The pieces fell into place. And the anger grew to rage. "The fight...?"

He nodded. "I did everything I could to get you to see I wasn't worth your time." A rueful curl edged up a corner of his lip.

"You did a really good job." The words hurled during their shouting match three years ago echoed back. "None of that was true? What about your fiancée?" He'd tossed that one out, a contract since he'd been a cub, and one he had to honor—he'd said. "Was that real or did you make her up too?" She leaned forward and stabbed a finger toward him. "Or are you married to her now?"

Color tinged his tawny cheeks. "Nadine? Yeah. I mean no. I didn't make her up. And no, I'm not married. I went back and told her pack I couldn't honor the contract because I loved someone else." He lifted his chin. "Because I love *you*."

Her heart blew open the box she'd kept it in, grabbed her emotions, and began to run. Giddiness rushed in and took over all thought. He loved her. Loved *her*. Then sanity returned to toss cold water on her happiness. He *said* he loved her. But he'd lied to her. Betrayed her love because of *his* insecurities. But her heart wouldn't let go of the ball so easily. She had her own insecurities, right? But the one inescapable truth couldn't be surmounted and her heart cried in protest.

She stepped up and looked him directly in the eye. "This won't work. You decided you knew what was best for me. And lied to make it happen. I wasn't a child, Nathan. And I refuse to be treated like one." With each word in the last sentence, her spine stiffened. "I'll get Alannah to find someone else if I have to."

She stepped around him and paced to the window. "Anyone else would be better than you."

# CHAPTER 6

He'd apologized and admitted he loved her and she didn't want to have anything to do with him. That's not how Nathan had imagined this going. A squawk from Nathan's back pocket heralded Suds' voice. "Burgers inbound. ETA two minutes."

Damn the interruption. He'd have gladly foregone food if he could've continued working this out, because she couldn't mean it. She still had feelings for him—she'd said she loved him three years ago, and her reaction when he was close now practically screamed it.

She stopped at the window, still as a baby deer in the underbrush.

Her frozen posture grabbed his attention. "Carrie—"

Max's sharp barks came to his ears.

Carrie sprinted the few steps to the back door and yanked it open.

"Wait. No." He pushed the button on the phone to talk to his team member and started running after her, in only his socks, the same as her. "Suds, get in here. Leave everyone else on perimeter." He shoved the phone in its pocket then drew the automatic from its holster at the small of his back. The screen door slammed behind him and he gained ground on Carrie, but she still reached the barn a good ten yards ahead of him.

Her scream curdled his stomach like rancid boudin and he flew across the remaining distance expecting to find Frazier inside. Yet again, Nathan had been too stupid, too late.

He skidded to a stop inside the open sliding door, colliding with Carrie. To keep her from toppling, he wrapped one arm around her.

He pulled her into an empty stall. Knelt down in the hay-strewn floor behind the wood jamb. Blood and coyote reek assaulted his senses like the fucker pissed everywhere. He could be hiding anywhere in the barn and Garrett's nose would be useless, even in wolf form.

He peeked around the jamb. On the opposite end of the barn and across the central breezeway, a sheep had been nailed up on the tack room's wall, front legs spread wide like a human when nailed to a cross. Pansy's remaining leg hung free. Coagulated blood trailed from its slit throat, through its fleece, down its eviscerated body. Flies already buzzed and crawled over a scene minutes old by the bright blood pooled beneath it. He pulled back into the stall.

Fury buzzed in his veins. If he killed as a wolf, he went for the neck. A quick snap and the animal didn't suffer. Even from a predator's standpoint, what had been done to the sheep surpassed barbaric. He shoved away the idea of how upset it would make Carrie. He dumped his emotions into a box and slammed the lid.

Time to go to work.

With one hand he motioned behind him for Carrie to stay put, then he set off to clear the small building. Stalls lined either side, six on one side, four on the other, all half wooden walls with metal bars continuing to the ceiling. It took less than a minute to ensure none of the empty pens concealed Frazier. Where were the menagerie of special needs animals she usually kept here?

He crept back and slid shut the door he'd entered to control who had access. The squeak echoed through the building, but it couldn't be avoided. The one at the other end remained open. He tucked the gun at the small of his back and stooped down.

Carrie's back rested on the wooden boards and her arms hugged her knees to form as small a ball as possible. Wide, brown eyes gleamed in the deepening darkness.

He tucked a wisp of hair behind her ear. If Garrett hadn't left the barn, he might be able to hear a conversation. Nathan used his fingers and hand to crudely sign while he mouthed 'If you hear me fighting, run, okay?'

She nodded, eyes wide and luminous.

Relief washed through him that although terrified, she could at least focus. He spun out of the stall and crept toward the tack room, sighting down the gun's barrel. Despite the probable futility, he stopped and tried his sense of smell again. The overwhelming smell of dung, blood, and Frazier made the gesture useless. The tack room remained unchecked, its door held shut with a metal hook fitted into an eyebolt. Unless the *rougarou* had gained a mage's skills or could manipulate metal like a fae, he wouldn't have been able to lock himself in the room.

Nathan approached the wooden panel, gun still pointed as if it were a threat. A trickle of blood slid out underneath the jam, streamed to join the pool at the base of the sheep. *Fuck. Fuck. Fuck.* He slipped the hook from the bolt and swung the door open. He jumped back as a small wave of red dumped over the threshold. Despite the setting sun, enough light remained so he didn't have to flip on the room's overhead.

Ripped apart animal carcass piled on eviscerated animal carcass piled on shredded animal carcass. From the mass, some chickens, a goat and a small donkey were identifiable by their heads, ten animals maybe. All slaughtered for no good reason and shoved in here.

Fury slammed through him. He fought the urge to shift. Controlled breaths helped him force the sprouting fur, teeth and claws back. He closed the door and latched it. Nathan telling her Frazier murdered any of her animals would be enough. There was no reason for her to see the carnage.

How had the *rougarou* gotten through? Baagh's wolves had arrived as Carrie had prepared her salad. They'd briefed and set up the security plan, then dispersed to their posts ringing the property. They'd have said something if they saw anything suspicious.

To cover all the bases, he pulled his mobile phone from his back pocket then punched the glowing app button. "Report."

"Suds," his team member's voice said through the phone. "I'm at the garage, where are you?"

"Barn. Clear the house." The coyote could've snuck into the house after he and Carrie ran out. "The rest, report."

The remainder checked in with no activity, as he'd figured. "Ten-Four," he said over the radio app. "Be on the lookout, Frazier has been in the barn." All acknowledged.

Somehow the damn coyote got on the property and created this horror while he and Carrie had been in the house. Snuck in and snuck out. Nathan pulled up short. This was less than an hour old, and a helluva lot of work. He had to be working with someone.

Or someones.

He again opened his senses, but the blood and coyote piss overwhelmed everything else, including Carrie's scent. Chip, his tracker and a member of his inbound team, should be able to sort this out. Though many in his clan and a couple on the team thought a female needed to stay at home and make wolf cubs, Chip's nose surpassed even his last tracker. He had no illusions. The petite wolf had way too much talent to waste and the rest could hang. He'd employ her and all her restless anger. The additional three inbound could help shore up the perimeter, but right now he'd need more help.

Nathan punched a number he'd called earlier.

"Baagh."

"You better get over to Carrie's place."

"What the hell now?" Frustration vibrated through the connection.

"I'll tell you when you get here. Don't need anyone listening in. And bring about ten of your team members and a stock trailer, too."

"My phone is *not* tapped." He gusted a breath. "It'll take me a bit. More than an hour."

"Fine." Nathan ended the call, then tapped another contact.

"Nathan," Alannah Johnson said, her whiskey-rasp instantly identifiable. "I'm actually on my way. E-T-A fifteen minutes. You better have a good reason why y'all didn't tell me about Frazier." The line went dead.

The perils of dealing with a clairvoyant. Or had someone squealed? Regardless, there may be hell to pay for not telling her about the coyote, but he'd pay any cost if she could help Carrie.

He crossed to the stall with leaden feet. She'd take this hard. Maybe even harder than she'd take her own death. He stepped onto the hay lining.

"They're dead, aren't they?" She rocked, arms still wrapped around her knees. Her eyes flashed to his, hard and dark. "Garrett killed them, didn't he?"

Words failed in the face of her anguish. He cleared his throat. "Let's go to the house, *chere*," he said in the tone he'd use to ease an animal. He extended his hand to help her to stand.

She slapped his hand away, a snarl on her lips. "Don't you fucking '*chere*' me. Answer me. Did he kill them?"

Frustration with his failure burned in his gut. "Some."

The hardness deep in her eyes shattered. Her keening cry cut him to the bone.

He sat next to her on the hay and gathered her into his arms.

A punch, then another, and another hit his body. They hurt. Bad. But he'd take all she could give. What was physical pain in the face of such suffering? He'd heal, but it would never bring back the animals she loved. She took on the special cases, those that probably would've been put down, like the three-legged sheep. She wanted them to have a good life. Cheese had given him regular reports. It's where the majority of her money went. Why she couldn't afford a new truck, one that didn't have reliable A/C. Why she hadn't moved after Frazier's judgement. She couldn't afford anything else, because she gave everything to those less fortunate than her.

Soon enough, her fury turned to exhaustion, leaving her sobbing, curled into a ball in his lap.

He stroked her hair, murmured soothing words. Not being able to do shit when someone was hurting made his insides twist. White-hot fury blasted through him, for her, for the animals, for the people Frazier murdered. But he couldn't lash out like his wolf craved. She needed him. He stood, bringing

her with him, then carried her to the house where Suds held
open the door.

He placed her on the couch as if she were paper-thin glass.
She hugged her knees again, tears tracking down her pale face.

As he moved to sit on the sofa, his phone squawked. He
removed it from his back pocket, then sat next to her, wrapped
his arm around her and pulled her close. Her body tensed.

Chase, one of the loaner team, said, "I've got Alannah John-
ston at the front gate. What? Ma'am. Please. Gimme that back."

Static, then a muffled female voice said, "Stop your crying.
I've got heels bigger than your dick."

Nathan huffed a laugh.

Alannah's voice turned clear and sickly sweet. "Nathan, can
you tell this miserable excuse for a chihuahua that as NAC
Minister I can go anywhere I damn well please, including
coming to see a good friend?"

Nathan muffled a laugh and tapped the talk button. "Only if
you give Chase back his phone."

"Chase? Why would anyone call him Chase? Does he have a
fetish for tennis balls? Nevermind. Don't want to know. Here."

"Sir?"

Nathan couldn't keep the smile from his face. "Let her
through."

"Yes, sir." For a six-foot eight wolf shifter, he sure sounded
like one whupped puppy.

"And Chase?"

"Sir?"

"I won't tell anyone your dick's that small."

"You're all heart, sir."

# CHAPTER 7

Murdered.

He'd murdered them. Pansy. Who knows how many more, since Nathan hadn't allowed her to see the scene.

Murdered.

The wail started small, and swelled like a bomb explosion for all the hearts and souls that had been extinguished. For no reason other than to hurt her.

Murdered.

She'd known the minute she'd walked through the barn door. The hum of their feelings had been diminished. If she hadn't been distracted by Nathan, she'd have known when it happened. Caught their fear. Maybe she could've caught Garrett. Could've killed him.

The scream hovered in her throat. She swallowed it, fury burning everything it touched to cinders until it reached her heart. Nothing remained. Nothing left.

Except Garrett. Garrett remained. How? He had a life once. He'd wasted it. Now? He'd come back to wreak havoc. No more. He couldn't continue. What had her love gotten those animals, all of whom had relied on her to keep them safe? To give them a good life? Nothing. She couldn't protect them against the hate of the Pure Paranormal Campaign. Why had she thought she could?

The front door opened and an unusually massive, silver-haired fae entered, one of Alannah's security team. Alannah practically rode the elf's heels, striding around him and into the room.

"Ma'am..."

Only about half his size, even in her four-inch heels, she waved the fae off. "If Nathan's here, the room's secure." She moved forward, a mask of concern on her face. "Carrie, I'm so sorry. Are you doing okay?"

From her seat on the couch, Carrie fought to keep her emotions reined, the least of which was betrayal that this woman only became her friend because of Nathan. "Thank you. I'm fine."

Perceptive swirling green-gold eyes narrowed. "No. You're not." She plunked her oversized designer purse on the coffee table and crossed her arms. "You're angry and—"

The back door burst open and she spun to face it, while Nathan shoved her back with one hand, and drew his gun with the other.

Suds, a seven-foot-tall wolf shifter with ebony skin and piercing amber eyes, entered. He held a limp black, white, and red ball of fur in his arms.

The wave of pain assaulted her senses and Carrie's heart stopped.

Max.

The world slowed. Someone kept saying "no, no, no." Then she realized the voice was her own.

A whine came from Suds' arms and Carrie's heart started again. She leapt from the couch. Max couldn't die. "Come on."

She raced toward the front door, only to be halted by Suds', "Nathan?"

Fury so sharp it pierced her soul shot through her. He wouldn't decide what to do. He'd done it before and look where it got him. She pointed her finger at Suds. "That's *my* damn dog. Don't you ask him for permission." She continued on her way to her trailer then skidded at the door as the fae held up a corded arm to block her path.

"I'm going with her." Nathan said, forestalling a confrontation.

The fae withdrew his arm and Carrie rushed out the door with Suds behind her. Nathan sprinted ahead with his natural wolf speed, opened the trailer and jumped inside after the two entered.

She flipped on the generator. Next, she flicked open the latch on the exam table and let the hydraulic arms bring it down. "Put her there," she said to Suds.

Carrie ripped open drawers and cabinets for supplies then turned to her best friend. She froze. The dog who'd been abused, the emaciated, whipped animal she coaxed out from behind the dumpster at the Sack Shack grocery, the very girl who'd blossomed into a confident dog, lay motionless on the stainless steel.

Blood from dozens of puncture wounds covered half her coat, she gasped, sides quivering, two of her limbs at unnatural angles, blood seeping from one closed eye.

*I can't do this.* Carrie's hands shook with the love for Max. Someone—something—had savaged her dog.

Garrett.

"You can do this, Carrie." Her head swiveled to Nathan, who stood beside her. "What can I do to help?" he asked.

His calm words slowed her panicked thoughts. She inhaled, centered, then got to work. A quick physical exam said the puncture wounds would have to wait. Based on the amount of damage, x-rays first. As she'd thought, the much larger animal had caused a collapsed lung and one of the bites punctured Max's spleen and intestines. Panic started to rise, but she shoved it back.

Max would not die. Not today. Not from *him*.

Plan her treatment as she had the neighbor's dog. The breaks, both clean and in the middle of the bones, could wait. Surgery on the organs first, then the eye, then the lacerations. Bones last. She took a deep breath and dove in.

An hour—or had it been hours?—later, she clipped the thread on the final suture and stepped back to survey her work. Max now had less fur than shorn skin, a huge bandage covering her right eye where nothing filled the socket any longer. The white gauze bandage continued over her ear where it had been almost torn off and Carrie had sewn it back together. Another bandage covered her middle from the internal repairs. Two casts supported bones that would knit together.

Carrie glanced at Nathan, who'd turned out to be a very capable surgical vet tech. "Thank you." Her voice carried the tremble of emotions she'd walled off. It couldn't crumble yet.

His strong arms encircled her, threatening to break the dam. She laid her head in the crook of his neck and struggled to get the tumult under control. Her gazed strayed back to Max.

By some miracle, the pup still lived. The deep tears at the dog's neck suggested she'd been grabbed there and shaken violently, something a predator did to its prey to break its spine, crush its windpipe, or sever a carotid artery. None of that had happened.

The wall she'd placed around her emotions burst and fat tears filled her eyes. She dashed at them with her forearm and made the rest return to their wells. It was up to fate now.

She disengaged from Nathan then laid her hands on the bandaged body, closed her eyelids and gave two heart-felt prayers, one of appreciation that Max had not been killed by the evil coyote, and one of supplication that her friend would heal and continue to live a good life.

"Well spoken."

She lifted her lids to find Alannah's fae bodyguard, hunched over on the opposite side of the exam table. Her amazement the guard remained—she glanced at the clock— two and a half hours later, was as strong as the fact he seemed to read minds.

He held up his hands. "Alannah asked that I help you. May I?" With Carrie's nod, he positioned one palm on Max's head, nearly engulfing it with his massive size. He placed his other hand midway down her side. The sinfully long, dark lashes swept to his cheeks and he began a low chanting. Not merely a mind-reader, a healer as well. A prickly energy danced on Carrie's skin as the elf's hands began to glow gold. The aura spread across Max's still limp body, then faded. The healer opened his eyes and removed his hands from the dog. "It's up to the Gods now." He jerked a nod and started down the trailer's stairs.

The enormity of his gift weighed on her. "Wait."

He hesitated but didn't turn.

The enormity of what she was about to say weighed on her. "Thank you. I am in your debt. May I know what you are called?"

"The debt is not yours. You may call me Simon," he said then continued into the night.

All energy drained from her. She swayed and propped her hand against a cabinet, not wanting to look at the chaos surrounding the operating table. It'd have to be cleaned. Her shoulders slumped.

"Let's go." Nathan's words snagged her attention. "You've done enough today to last anyone a year."

She shook her head and carefully gathered Max in her arms. "My mess, my cleanup. Could you hold Max's IV?"

Two people, one male, one female, stepped up into the trailer. Both wore scrubs with the NAC logo on the left breast.

*What now?* "Can I help you?"

The female's brunette ponytail danced around her shoulders when she shook her head in the negative. "We're here to help *you*."

"What?" Carrie's gaze swung between Nathan and the pair.

The male said, "Alannah sent us. She said you had a hard day and wouldn't go to bed before you cleaned up your trailer. We're here to do it for you."

"But you won't know where stuff goes. How I—"

"Carrie," Nathan said. "Let them do it. You're barely upright. You can reorganize your things in the morning." His seductive words coaxed her from the trailer and into the house, despite her OCD tendencies.

The living room had gotten a lot more crowded than when she'd left, but the exhaustion dragged at her. No time for introductions. She continued through to her bedroom where Max had a soft-orthopedic bed on the floor. Since the pup was still under the anesthesia, Max didn't whimper as Carrie laid her out carefully, then accepted the half-full IV bag from Nathan and hung it from the knob of her nightstand to ensure it continued with gravity. The poor dog would be too woozy until morning for Carrie to have to worry about the cone of shame.

The bed beckoned, but she had people in her house. Hopefully she could manage five minutes of social niceties.

Four shifters had joined Suds in her living area. Two she recognized. One of the two she didn't know caught her attention. Who ever heard of a female escaping the notoriously backward view on a wolf shifter female's place in the world?

"You remember Uno, right?" Nathan said, pulling Carrie's attention away from the woman.

"Carrie." The freckled redhead saluted her with the knife he'd been polishing. Though Uno easily topped six feet and didn't lack in the muscles department, next to the rest of the shifter males, he seemed small. Usually, he more than made up for the difference in attitude and sarcasm.

"How could I forget," she said drily. The shifter wielded a blade as if he'd been born with it in his paw. He'd told her once guns made too much noise. "Good to see you again."

"And Mouse," Nathan continued.

The black-haired man dipped his chin. "Sorry to see you under these circumstances, ma'am."

Since Mouse made it a practice to speak only when absolutely necessary, that he had given her so many words made her heart swell. "It's Carrie, if you remember, and there isn't a circumstance I'd not be happy to see you." She meant every word.

"This is Fuzzy, my explosives expert."

The dark-haired shifter's face tightened almost imperceptibly, then his grin grew to show dang near every white tooth in his arsenal, as deliberate and insincere a display as she'd ever seen. "Nice to meet you, Carrie." His voice carried hints of the bedroom, but what emotions she could sense from him made her feel as if she'd be the last one he'd ever bed. She had no time for those say-one-thing-and-mean-another games.

"And this is Chip. She's my nose."

Chip's hands were planted on slim hips above her long, long legs encased in jeans, and lightweight black combat boots completed her look. "Why do I always get last billing?" Her tone carried the barest tinge of snarl.

"Because he saved the best for last?" Carrie said. All of Nathan's team had nicknames, some known only to the group. It wasn't hard to understand where Chip got hers.

The female shifter's tawny gaze swung to Carrie, looked her up and down. The echo of emotion matched her dismissive tone. "Sure."

"Suds, you know the plan. Brief and deploy." Nathan swung toward Carrie's bedroom.

His team's eyes tracked him, then turned to her, speculation rampant. Heat bloomed in her cheeks. Nothing left but to follow him. Little stings pricked the soles of her feet.

*Geez.* She'd even forgotten she didn't have boots on and ran across a patch of sand burs in the yard. Sure, the socks caught most, but some of the evil little things made it through. In the background, the whoosh of the shower called like a siren. If she didn't do it now, she'd fall in bed all gross from the day.

No sign of Nathan, despite the shower's activity, not that she wasn't so tired she cared at this point. She stripped down and walked naked into the hot spray. The comforting water beat on the bunched muscles of her back while she leaned her hands on the tiled wall.

The door opened and *snicked* shut behind her.

She tensed, sensing Nathan had entered behind her. But her exhaustion silenced any protest.

Warm, soapy hands stroked her body, long and sure,

relaxing her tight muscles. His strong fingers attacked her hair next, stripping the elastic from it, then sudsing. She started to drift off with the massage. He could make millions at a hair salon. She bit down on a moan.

His fingers stilled. "Did you say somethin'?"

"Uh, no." Her voice sounded more frog than human.

His fingers resumed their magic, then he rinsed her hair. A soft toweling off followed. As if she were in a trance, her body couldn't move, only keep her upright by the barest margin. His arms scooped her up and she curled herself against his warmth.

He placed her on the bed, pulled the covers over her. The gentle kiss on her forehead was the last thing she remembered.

# CHAPTER 8

"Not just Frazier. A fae, too?" Nathan strove to keep his tone low.

The sun had barely promised daylight on the horizon. He'd been unable to sleep. Since putting Carrie to bed around midnight, he'd been going through all the leads on the coyote's reappearance. Something kept telling him more to this lay hidden in the mud of information. When Chip and Uno rolled in with the news, it seemed too good to be true.

"No. It was Tinkerbell's baby-fresh scent," Chip rolled her eyes and crossed her arms. "This nose doesn't lie, not when blood's been spilled." While the best tracker he'd ever seen, maybe that ever lived, her arrogance and anger often rubbed people the wrong way. Especially within the wolf community.

"I'm sorry for her dog, but if the pup hadn't defended the animals and chased after the attackers, we wouldn't have known."

*Whoa.* Easily the nicest comment she'd made in the year she'd worked for him. And with the barest sliver of approval, too.

"It took me a while," Chip continued. "But a single drop mingled with Carrie's dead animals. Garrett's scent was so strong in the barn, I almost missed it. Damn coyote must've saved up his piss for days to spread that much around." Her lip curled in distaste. "The elf's scent traveled with Frazier across the property to where they breeched the spell."

"No fae could've managed that." The fingers on Uno's right hand tapped the handle of the blade strapped at his thigh. "That means he's working with at least two others and someone who could breach Carrie's cousin's spell. My vote is for Clan Magic."

Chip's brow crunched together. "I almost discounted what my nose was telling me. I thought he inspired other immortals, but did his work solo."

Nathan began to weigh variables. "It's a departure from prior M-O. I'd been kickin' around the idea it's not really Frazier, but if your nose says it is, it's enough for me."

She shifted and something alien flitted across her face —doubt.

"What?"

"Well, I first thought I imagined it." She started to pace, her frown deepening. "Maybe something in his cologne or the fabric softener he used, or maybe even something he ate coming out of his pores, like feta or garlic, but I'm getting something different than the clothing you gave me." She pivoted and stopped at the far end of the living area. "It's the same. But not."

The idea they weren't dealing with Garrett Frazier, once the seed of a hunch, took root. "Keep on it."

Carrie appeared from the bedroom dressed in jeans and another plaid snap-shirt. "Morning," she mumbled as she made her way to the coffee pot. "What's she talking about?"

He entertained not telling her, but trying to do what he

thought best for her caused him to leave his mate three years ago and lose her love. She'd never forgive him if he did it again. "We're working on the idea it may not be Frazier."

The stream of coffee stopped. Carrie carefully replaced the pot in the machine, then screwed the lid on her travel cup. "I guess that matches with the weird feeling I got from whoever was in the shed yesterday." She shrugged and crossed to the bench at the front door, where she sat, leaned over, and grabbed her work boots.

Too calm. "Where are you going?"

Carrie shoved her foot into a boot. "I've got customers to see today."

He teased the hint of determination from otherwise tone-less words. "I thought we went through this last night." Nathan's frustration spiked, probably caused by his lack of sleep, and he tried to grab hold of it.

Carrie paused from sliding on her second boot. "We did. And I need to get to my appointments." She pushed her foot down, settled her jeans over the leather shaft, then stood. "You can come if you like or not. Your choice."

How had she pushed him into this corner? Short of tying her up, he had no option.

"Besides, I'm your bait, right? You want to catch Garrett or whoever is doing this? Here's your opportunity." She yanked the door open and plunged into the still-dark morning.

Dammit. He followed her and ducked into the trailer.

"Holy crap," she said. "They really did clean up." She lowered the latch on the exam table, ran her hand over the smooth surface. Bent down to peer across the steel. "Spotless." She re-secured the stainless slab then moved to her equipment drawers. One after another she yanked them open then slammed them shut. "How...?" Her mouth hung open.

"Sorcerers," he said. "They must've done a cleaning spell." For a fleeting moment, the idea to lock her inside the trailer flitted through his brain, but he discounted it as quickly as it came.

"Huh." She shook her head and pushed past him out the door.

He swore under his breath, then followed her. "At least tell me where we're headed."

She pulled her mobile phone from her back pocket. "Absolutely. You want me to send you my calendar?"

The icy tone chilled him. "Sure." It wouldn't pay to continue the fight. He lost this round and she knew it.

A sad, twisted smile appeared on her mouth. "Thank you. I need to work to keep this off my mind." She stopped, as if she would say more, then shook her head. "We leave in fifteen." She tapped on her phone, then spun and disappeared back into the house.

While she readied for her day, he briefed the crew. Chip, Fuzzy, Uno and two of Baagh's loaners would come with them on the appointments. Suds, Mouse and three of the loaners would remain on patrol at the house. He'd considered leaving behind all of the Security Chief's team at the house, because they needed a safe base of operations, but the risk was too high Frazier would make a run for Carrie while on the road.

He climbed into the passenger seat at her honk. The crew would loosely bookend her, one SUV in front, the other behind. Cheese would work the sites up in the background, trying to make up for lost prep time.

All of Cheese's efforts proved futile. By the time they pulled back into her driveway, he wasn't merely sweaty, but covered in Central Texas dirt. Carrie's stamina, both mentally and physically, stunned him. How did she do everything? She'd been banged around by cattle, almost kicked by a stallion she'd been getting ready to neuter. And when she had to tell someone her cat had bladder cancer too advanced to operate, a lump grew in his throat when the woman broke down and sobbed, hanging onto Carrie like a lifeline.

"We'll check in with Suds to coordinate perimeter," Uno said as the security detail passed by him and filed into the house.

Carrie had gone back into the trailer to inventory her supplies, their replenishment testament to a busy day. As the hours had progressed, her attitude toward him disintegrated, to the point where she spoke to him not at all.

Dammit. Garrett should've made a run at her today. He had every opportunity, even with the team watching her. Nathan banked on the *rougarou's* desperation to trip him up and make him try, even though the moment wasn't opportune. It should've worked. Garrett always struck within a day of his warning. The shed and her animals could only be those warnings. Now that they had the property buttoned up, witch-wards strengthened, this should be the least of Nathan's worries.

His phone rang and he removed it from his back pocket. He walked out into her front yard, but kept an eye on the open trailer door. "Baagh. I never got to say thanks for removing the animals from the barn and cleaning up. I don't know if she could've handled that."

"Sure." Baagh paused. "We got a tip. Garrett's supposed to be holed up in a town called Stonewall."

Nathan stilled. "Stonewall." That was on the other side of Enchanted Rock from Carrie, maybe forty miles. He'd have bet Frazier wouldn't have been more than a couple of miles away, tops. He always stayed close to observe his victims. Any break in MO concerned Nathan.

"One of my own staff saw him enter a house." Baagh must've

heard the question Nathan tried to keep from his tone. "He's had it under surveillance since then and there's been no movement."

A witness changed things, right? He'd have suspected an anonymous tip. "You've started an operation to capture him?"

"That's the problem. Because of this, I've had to deploy my most experienced men to protect our own leadership. Plus, NAC Security asked for additional personnel for *their* senior leadership."

Nathan braced for the security chief's next words.

"I need you and your team for this."

*Merde.* Even expected, the words made his gut tighten. "You know it's a trap."

"I'm trusting you to figure out a way through it."

Nathan put the call on speaker and activated the mapping app on the phone to scan for possible meet locations. Ah, a town next to Stonewall. "Tell your team we'll meet at...Hye. There's a post office there. Say an hour. Send me the address of the house and I'll get Cheese on it."

"We've done the background. The county owns it now for back taxes."

"Send it anyway." Clan Security usually did a good job, but Cheese would do better.

"Very well. They'll be there at eight." Baagh signed off.

"Where are you going?"

Nathan lifted his gaze from his phone to Carrie, who'd propped her shoulder on the trailer door's jamb. He didn't like leaving her here with less protection than before, but if they had an opportunity to get Frazier, they had to take it. "Baagh believes they may have Frazier cornered in Stonewall."

"Surely it's a trap." She wrapped her arms around her middle. "Do you...trust Sai?"

"Yes. I trust him. We've been in tough scrapes in the past. Even he thinks it's likely a trap. But we have a sighting and we have to take a chance." He did trust Baagh, right? Right. The best way to defeat an enemy was to make them distrust each other. Nathan couldn't buy into it.

She nibbled on her lower lip, and her shoulders hunched. "But if you *know* it's a trap..."

He crossed to her. "That's the best way to defeat it." When the concern lingered in her eyes, he said, "I'm not taking everyone with me. With the added protection spells from your cousins, and the five wolves I'm leaving behind, you should be safe."

"Is that why you think I'm worried?" She snorted a disbelieving laugh. "You wouldn't leave me here if you thought I wasn't safe. The last time you faced Frazier, you almost died."

"I'll just make sure I win again."

She lifted a hand to cup his cheek and he reveled in the promise of her finger's soft caress. For moments their gazes tangled, her mouth opened as if to say something, but shut again. Her fingers faltered, fell away as she turned from him. "Good luck."

The soft, sad words cut through him. "Carrie?"

She stopped but didn't turn.

Suddenly the scant ten feet could've been a million. "I love you."

Her ponytail bobbed with her head nod. She sniffed and continued toward the house. The front door shut with a quiet click.

# CHAPTER 9

Carrie plopped down next to Max and folded her legs under her on the tile floor. She stroked the dog's chin under the cone, relieved to still have her. Carrie wanted to pick up her best friend and cuddle, but the injuries prevented that.

She checked her phone. Another hour and she'd give Max her last round of meds for the day. At least the dog's injuries seemed to be healing well.

Minutes ago, Carrie had taken the pup outside to go to the bathroom, and the poor girl wobbled on her two good legs. Max would get better.

*Had* to get better.

Carrie moved to her own bed as a horrible pit of loss grew in her gut for those poor animals put through such pain, undoubtedly terrified. At least he hadn't killed them all. Carrie could only assume Max chased many of them out while Garrett slaughtered others. She shivered and turned her thoughts elsewhere. Let Max get back to full strength and she could cry her eyes dry.

She pulled her laptop from the bed and stared at her supply order. The screen swam in a jumble of numbers and letters.

Why had Nathan gone? It had been a trap as sure as she was a Leftover. She'd almost begged him not to go. He wouldn't have left if he'd thought he didn't have a good chance.

At least that's what she kept telling herself between bouts of mental ass kicking for the way she'd responded to his words. Or not responded. But he'd only said he loved her. Not that she was his mate. What if someone else came along? One whom his wolf wouldn't deny?

His kind couldn't live without their mates. A pit yawed in her heart.

Tires screeched outside. They were back. *Thank the Gods.* She put her laptop aside and slid off the bed. The front door banged at the same time a controlled panic assaulted her senses.

Carrie raced from her bedroom into the living area where Uno and Fuzzy carried in an enormous black wolf. Its fur glimmered wet in too many places. Blood dripped red across the floor. Behind them, Chip slammed the door shut.

Her mouth dried as she counted those who returned. "Where's Nathan?"

"Disappeared."

"What do you mean?" Her blood turned to ice.

"We can't find him. I think that's what disappeared means." Chip pushed back chairs from Carrie's dining room table and swept a pair of silver candle sticks from its top. Laid the wolf down diagonally on the table and its muzzle still cleared the edge.

No. Not Nathan. She took several steps back, as if the distance could change things. If only the wolf in front of her could be him. He was almost the right size, yet a bit smaller.

Definitely the wrong color, though. Nathan's shifted form had golden brown sides and muzzle with a white stomach, a darker top, and a streak up the nose. That left... "Is-is that Suds?"

"Yeah." Chip said. "He wouldn't fit on your exam table, so we brought him in here. What do you need from your trailer?"

The amount of blood pooling on the table top meant she'd need about everything—anesthesia tanks, pulse/ox monitor too. At least he had enough control to maintain his wolf form. The transformation back to human would probably have been fatal.

"Come with me." She ran for her supplies with Chip and Uno nipping at her heels. She loaded them down with the necessities, grabbed her surgical bag, and scooped up even more gauze and bandages.

When they returned to the dining room, Fuzzy lay across Suds's middle, stretching his arms from head to tail. Weak, yet still threatening, growls came from the injured shifter. "Hurry. He's trying to get back up."

"Hold his muzzle still," Carrie said.

Chip stepped forward. "Hey, buddy. You need to chill a bit. We're gonna get you fixed up."

For a moment, Carrie halted her preparations, transfixed at Chip's soft, soothing tone. The female shifter's fingers slid across the massive wolf's cheeks, stroked the dark fur with unexpected tenderness. The beast settled as if transfixed by the gentle words and caresses. Carrie shook off her surprise and got back to work.

Suds's blue eye tried to focus on her as she placed the anesthesia cup around his muzzle. "It's okay. I'll fix you up right and you'll be back in no time. Promise. But you're going night-night for a while."

Probably only due to the anesthesia, Suds shut his eye as if he trusted her to do her best. And she would. For Nathan's sake. She shoved her worry about him to the back of her mind. She needed every ounce of concentration to make sure she didn't miss anything.

Once she'd intubated Suds, she performed an examination. He appeared to have sustained several gunshots, and...a sword thrust through the side? *Dammit.*

"Call Baagh and get him to send his best healer. Suds is going to need one." She crossed to the kitchen and began to scrub. When no one moved, she glanced at the trio, all of whom traded looks with each other. "What?"

"We were set up," Uno said. "We can't trust Sai Baagh."

Carrie's phone chirped its announcement of a text. "Someone pull the phone from my back pocket."

Without hesitation, Chip marched forward to perform the task. The locked screen displayed the text, "Alannah said, 'Healer on the way.'"

Carrie snorted a small laugh. As if she should've expected any different. She dried her hands with a sterile towel and set to work.

Multiple stab and bite wounds added to the total. More than once she caught herself wondering how a body could take all the trauma. At least the sword thrust and bullets hadn't severed his spine or penetrated his heart, only broke several ribs, entered one of Suds' lungs, and hit his intestines. Long, messy work to get it all back together. Thank the Gods for a shifter's healing abilities.

By the time she closed on the final wound several hours later, she'd blown through all of her spare blood supplies. Uno had already given a transfusion and now Fuzzy donated. Chip, acting as Carrie's surgical assistant, would be next. Fortunately, Shifters didn't suffer from stupid human blood type and Rh-factor problems. Carrie would give her own blood after Chip, but her non-shifter essence wouldn't be as valuable as his clan's.

She unclipped the heart monitor from Sud's tongue, slid the tube from his throat, then stripped off her gloves. Mercifully, Suds still breathed on his own, though shallow, and his heart still beat, though thready.

A petite young woman garbed in black BDUs and combat boots stepped forward. Carrie noted her entering sometime earlier, but had to concentrate.

This sorcerer, one seeming to be barely out of her teens, was the best Alannah could send from the NAC?

Fuzzy jumped to his feet and Chip moved her hand to her knife, full protective mode engaged.

Thin, elegant hands waved them off. "You need not fear me, shifters." The soft tone carried a power that made the hair on the back of Carrie's neck rise. She gave the sorcerer who'd refused to give her name a second glance. Long, white hair braided to her butt belied her young appearance and size. Eyes so dark Carrie couldn't differentiate iris from pupil surveyed all with a confidence that spoke of knowledge and purpose.

Carrie moved back to give the sorcerer room to work. The healer had Suds in her hands now.

"You may want to move some of this back." The sorcerer nodded toward Carrie's bandages and supplies still on the table next to Suds. "And he won't need blood after this."

Carrie sent a quick prayer to the Gods it would be so. She unhooked Fuzzy and pressed a small adhesive bandage on the needle's entry. While Carrie dealt with the enormous shifter, Chip moved the paper-wrapped packages, tapes, and other items into the kitchen.

With quiet grace, the sorcerer closed her eyes and took a

deep breath. The mass of shorn and bandaged shifter came up to her shoulders. She put one hand on Sud's head, the other on his side over where his heart would be. Her lips began to move, and only after several seconds could Carrie detect the chanting of the sorcerer's spell. Script, ancient and unreadable, appeared in gold across the woman's skin. As the murmurs became louder, the writing's glow spread to surround her hands. The level grew louder, more commanding, and the aura spread to Suds as well. Power swirled around the room, buffeting them all, blowing Carrie's ponytail over her shoulder.

Good Gods. The electricity dancing on Carrie's skin gave the feeling of buzzing bees. A healing spell had never been this intense before.

A jagged streak of white light blinded Carrie, then *boom*.

She flew backward into the wall and crumpled. *What the...* Woozy, she scrabbled to pick herself up from the floor.

"Stay back. Wait for the glow to fade," the sorcerer shouted.

The words were muffled by the trauma to Carrie's eardrums. She finally staggered to her feet, hand shading her eyes from the intense white light surrounding Suds.

The healer clambered to her feet next to Carrie. The shifters rubbed their ears and shared uneasy gazes, but they held back. As long as they believed the sorcerer was helping. Chip pulled out her phone and punched the screen. "Stay at your posts."

The words were still muffled. Carrie poked her pinkie into her ear canal, then pulled it out. Good. No blood. She'd have to wait for the ringing to diminish. She surveyed the room and her stomach sank. The explosion blew out her windows and glass littered the floor. At least she had some plywood to cover them until she could get new ones. Dang it. Her finances were already stretched and now she'd have another big expense.

What did that matter? Suds would live, but Nathan had disappeared. They wouldn't have left him behind. *Dead?* The word slithered across her thoughts and struck like a cobra. She gasped for air. She'd been able to push the idea to the back of her mind while she worked on Suds. Now, the thought crushed her chest with the strength of a boa.

No. Not Nathan. Not now. Not the way she'd left their relationship, afraid to admit what she really felt. Afraid to tell him she loved him.

Tears began to gather. *Stop. Wait to fall apart until you're alone.* No need to confirm to all the immortals here that Leftovers were weak. Piece by shattered piece, she pulled herself back together while the glow around the shifter faded.

Finally, the aura covering Suds diminished and Carrie approached the table. "May I touch him?"

"Yes. I've done all I can do." Lines bracketed her mouth, a testament to the exhaustion the sorcerer would never admit. She pushed back the heavy weight of her hair, which had come loose from the blast. "It is in the hands of the Shifter gods, now." The healer's hair began to re-braid itself, finishing with the elastic securing the end.

"We thank you for the gift." Though she'd never seen one herself, Carrie suspected the spell had been something which took a large piece of the healer's own essence to accomplish. Once gone, it could never be replaced. A true wonder.

The woman's lips compressed into a flat line. "Thank Alannah." Her eyes shifted. "And your cousin."

By the edge of bitterness in the tone, Alannah and Carrie's cousin had spent some personal capital for this to happen by calling in a debt, and a large one at that. How could Carrie repay the favor?

The healer rooted around in a large tote she'd brought then

handed Carrie a black linen drawstring bag. "When he's healed enough to change, you can use this. Don't open the pouch until you are ready to use the spell. Then use the bag to shield your fingers and put the sphere between his eyes. The spell will work itself."

Carrie hefted the fabric bag in her palm. Unusually heavy. Her fingers outlined the smooth ball, about twice the size of a big marble. "Why does he need this?"

"He's been trapped as a wolf with magic. This will remove the spell." She frowned. "I think."

"What do you mean you think?" Fuzzy asked. A wolf's menacing growl rumbled in his tone.

Quick as lightening, the healer snatched the black bag back from Carrie. "Back off, Spot, or my magic and I will go home." Despite her size and the soft lilt of her voice, her squared posture, bent knees, and sneer meant business.

Carrie addressed the sorcerer. "Please excuse the insult. He's only worried for his friend. I'm grateful for any assistance you are willing to gift us." Carrie shot Fuzzy a prodding glare.

Fuzzy dropped his menacing stare and managed to appear contrite. "My apologies, Healer. We would, indeed, be grateful."

The woman's gaze shifted around the group of wolves. She tossed the bag back at Carrie.

Unprepared, Carrie's fingers bobbled the precious item. By the time she'd secured it, the front door slammed shut.

A low whistle sounded from Fuzzy. "And I thought you moved fast, Chip."

Chip's brows slammed together. "Shut it, furball. You almost caused us to lose the spell to get Suds back."

Fuzzy growled, low and angry.

Carrie jammed her hands on her hips, fear, frustration, and

despair filling her. "Dammit. Nathan could be dead for all we know, and all you two can do is pick at each other?"

"I didn't say Nathan was dead. I said he disappeared." Chip rolled her eyes. "Never count a wolf as dead until you see their body. And even then, don't be so sure."

Their belief caused her pulse to thrum. He wasn't dead. Or at least she'd believe that until proved otherwise. She pushed the negative emotions away, allowing only hope to remain. 'Work—the balm for a troubled mind', as her mother used to say. "If Nathan's still alive, we'll need to mount a rescue."

Surprise flitted across Uno's face, which turned to speculation. "To catch a coyote, you need a trap." Uno's fingers danced along the handle of the knife strapped at his thigh.

The nervous gesture signaled his unwillingness to ask. Maybe Nathan instructed them to keep her safe at all costs. Didn't matter why. Nathan needed a rescue. And she'd be damned if she'd be the reason why it didn't happen.

"You have the trap's perfect bait standing right here."

# CHAPTER 10

Nathan tested the bonds tying all four paws together. Probably enchanted, but even if not, thick enough he couldn't wriggle out or break them completely. Same for the binding around his muzzle.

He tried once again to shift back to his human form, despite the possible damage it could cause to his wrists and ankles. As before, pain lanced through his skull, a crushing vice that sent him spiraling toward oblivion. He ceased his attempt before he lost consciousness again.

For long moments he breathed heavily through his quivering nose, unable to pant. Something held him in his shifted form, a magic unknown to him. He suppressed his fury. He could barely breathe to begin with.

When he could open his eyes, he searched the small room once again for anything which could tell him of his prison and those who kept him captive. The single, bare bulb dangling from the ceiling illuminated the four dingy walls. No windows in the ten by ten room, but the scarred intricate moldings around the six-panel solid wood door said old home. Stained hardwood floors. The scent of blood and shit and piss combined each time he sucked in a breath. A holding area for prior prisoners? Not the same fifties ranch house he and his team had entered.

His wolf-keened hearing picked up footsteps coming his way.

Time to learn more about his captors. He ceased his struggles and lay still.

Elvish. They spoke the tongue of the high language.

He barely suppressed the feral growl. The coyote *was* working with others. Garrett once claimed he had supporters of all the clans, but wouldn't provide names or details. The speed of the coyote's trial and execution had always bothered Nathan. He'd assumed the clans wanted any possible publicity of Garrett's claims smothered to avoid more rallying around the Pure Paranormal Campaign banner. Now it seemed as if possibly the clan council members knew they had a problem and were covering it up. Betrayal lanced through him. He'd *thought* he could count on Clan Shifter. But with the betrayal in Stonewall, no one could be trusted.

The voices ceased as they came closer to the door. It wouldn't have mattered. Nathan didn't understand Elvish. But now he knew it to be two males. Plus, a third being who remained silent, but by the weight of the steps, also male.

The door opened and the three entered.

He'd tried to remain as if still in a drugged sleep, but his wolf reacted to the coyote's stench by instinct. He couldn't stop the snarl.

Frazier merely stared through him, as if Nathan's enormous wolf form wasn't bound at his feet, his to kill. As if Nathan were nothing.

Something tugged at him. He *looked* like Garrett Frazier, had the same long, whipcord body, topped with the same sandy brown hair held back from his face with a rubber band. The same amber eyes. The same smell of the *rougarou* he'd captured three years ago.

Almost.

Nathan couldn't put his nose exactly on the anomaly. Each time he tried, it slid away. But the subtle scent was enough for him to know this coyote shifter may look like Garrett Frazier, but wasn't. Nathan studied the two elves flanking him.

Both matched the standard elf profile, lean and elegant. The taller with dark blonde, the shorter with light, almost white hair, braids hanging on either side of his sneering face. Cold, hard violet stared back. By the level of disgust in them, Nathan should be buried somewhere by now. No time to worry why he still lived.

How had they done it? To get the same DNA, the same physical appearance, the same almost everything, because this wasn't Garrett Frazier. It was...

His identical twin.

Nathan's cousins, Julien and Jacques, were the same way, only the faintest scent differentiated them. *Merde*. He deserved to die for his stupidity. Coyote shifters were notorious for not obeying NAC rules dictating all clan births must be registered. Garrett had been born to a rogue family. That Frazier had appeared to have sprung from nowhere perpetrated the cult mythology amongst his followers. Pure Paranormal adherents may have gone underground with Frazier's death.

But his twin could inspire their boldness again.

Two from Clan Magic stepped into the room. Voluminous black robes with hoods completely obscured their bodies and faces. Interesting, since those types of robes were largely ceremonial. Today they must've worn them to hide their identities. Cowards.

Like physical features could ever hide them. He relied on his sense of smell. One male, one female. Yay. Betrayed by a Shifter. Elves and now sorcerers. All he'd need is a Demon, and all clans would be represented at this shitshow.

That Nathan still lived said he still had a purpose. Carrie had been alive when he left her—when—last night? It had to be to lure Carrie out. She wouldn't surrender herself for him, would she?

His stomach curdled. If she thought it would save him, of course she would.

"Hebert. You should not have come back," the shorter of the two elves said in the accented, halting tones of one who didn't speak English with regularity. "Now we can have two for one." He nodded to the sorcerers. "Get on with it."

Interesting. The elf's words spoke of retaliation. Retaliation spoke of messiness. Messiness added to the weight of this not being Frazier. The one thing the *rougarou* did right was careful deliberation, not disorganization. Precision had been his calling card, each scene orchestrated for maximum effect and maximum terror in the HP community.

Scenes flashed by, details he never should've discounted. He should've figured this out way before he reached Split. *Merde.* For someone known for his strategy prowess, he sure fucked this one up.

The sorcerers finished laying out their supplies and began by grabbing his head and tail, adjusting him, most likely, with a compass point. A growl built low in his throat, but they didn't react to its threat. Then they poured a thick circle of salt around him. More salt created designs within the heavy ring. With the last grain dropped, a fine power raised the fur across Nathan's body. They stood opposite each other, the male at Nathan's head, the female at his tail. The female started chanting, the words undecipherable. Minutes ticked by, then the male joined. Electricity began to spark over his coat like firecrackers, then dove into his body, live wires bouncing around inside. He couldn't stop the whimpers of agony ripped from his throat as his bones shrank, wolf's body compacted.

The chanting stopped.

The magic still zinged through his body like hornets, keeping the spell active. He was two hundred pounds of wolf stuffed in a seventy-pound pelt. Not enough room to breathe, organs scrunched, heart barely able to beat. Shallow breaths were all he could manage. He hurt from his brain to his nads. Even if he'd not been bound, he wouldn't have been able to move.

The female sorcerer dusted her hands on her robe. "You will tell her of our achievement?" Challenge echoed in the female's voice.

His altered eardrums may have muffled her words, but they came through loud and clear. *Her?*

The shorter of the two fae's mouth thinned in a parody of a smile. "He's perfect. You may leave."

The female paused. Probably because the elf dodged her question. The old adage never changed—no honor among thieves. He huffed a canine laugh.

The elf reared back to kick him.

Nathan braced for the impact aimed at his stomach.

"No," the male sorcerer yelled.

The sneering fae halted, fury twisting his pale, cold features. He whirled toward the taller of the shrouds.

"He's stuffed into this skin. If you kick him, he'll probably explode. Then you won't have him for this afternoon."

The elf's hands fisted and for a moment, he leaned forward like he would discount the sorcerer's words completely. Then the fingers unfurled and he stepped back. He waved a hand. "You may leave."

The larger elf exited the room behind the two sorcerers and reappeared seconds later with an unassembled large plastic dog kennel. The blond elf waved a hand at his companion. "Assemble it." He snapped his fingers and Not-Garrett followed him from the room.

*What the...* Not-Garrett hadn't uttered a word during this entire ordeal. Nathan had even forgotten the coyote was in the room. Someone else ran this show. The mysterious 'Her' referenced by the Clan Magic female.

Nathan could barely suppress the cry when the elf lifted him. The sorcerer had been right, he would explode. Once in the bottom of the crate, he could only concentrate on sucking air into cramped lungs. Black spots danced in his vision.

The elf made short work of assembling the carrier around him. Within minutes, the cage door clicked into place. "Hang in there, Hebert." The elf uttered a grim chuckle. "You've got a neutering to go to."

# CHAPTER 11

"I think that's it," Carrie murmured. "I don't think they bit on it."

"It ain't over yet." Uno's words filtered through the tiny device buried in her ear canal.

Carrie forced herself not to seek out the team's hiding spots to reassure herself of her safety. She collapsed the table, and moved to the one they'd put up under the other portable canopy as a recovery area. Carrie wiped the moisture at her brow and checked her phone. Three-fifteen. No more waiting or recovering patients remained under the two large, pop-up canopies Barry donated. Another half an hour remained in the time she'd posted for the free spay and neuter clinic.

"It looks like we're done." She said to Barry's niece.

MayLee paused from wiping down the portable prep table with antiseptic spray. "You sure?"

"Absolutely." Carrie hadn't needed to show the teen how to do something twice. Should she really wanted to be a vet, MayLee would have no problem. "If you ever want to go on calls with me, you're welcome to," Carrie said.

MayLee's smile could've lit up Times Square. She skirted around the table and hugged Carrie. "Thank you. I had so much fun."

"Even if it was hotter than the surface of the sun today?"

MayLee snorted a laugh and pulled at the front of her Split High School Wolves t-shirt out to fan herself. "Even if you got to work in the air-conditioned trailer and I had to work out here." She giggled.

Carrie joined her laughter. "Go on. I'll finish cleaning up."

"You sure?"

"I'm sure." Carrie fished fifty bucks from her back pocket and held it to the teen. "You were great."

Her raven ponytail swished around her shoulders. "I can't..." A glitter flashed in her eyes and her hand snaked out for the cash.

*Huh.* Barry was a gremlin but married a non-HP human over a century ago, eventually resulting in MayLee. If Carrie remembered rightly, MayLee's family tree stayed stubbornly in the non-immortal vein down several generations. How had the teen ended up a gremlin? Had they registered her with the NAC as one? Carrie shook her head. No telling. Gremlin genes were notoriously difficult to predict. Add that with a general feeling Council rules didn't work toward the benefit of everyone, not to mention all except the HPs had strict pecking orders within their clans, and you often ended up with rogue paranormals. Barry had been so good to her, it wasn't like Carrie would report them. 'Nunya', as in nunya business, seemed an appropriate way to treat the matter.

MayLee skipped off to her grandfather's garage across the street. Initially, Carrie worried about using her today. She'd explained the plan, such as it was, to Barry and promised to take his granddaughter on a farm call with her. Carrie should've known something was up with the crafty smile on his face when he'd said his granddaughter might be tougher than she looked.

Carrie couldn't get a grasp on any toughness residing in the sixteen-year old MayLee—slim, of average height, and dressed in shorts and a t-shirt. An average teen. Despite her best efforts, Barry and MayLee insisted. Carrie did get the teen's promise she'd bolt at the merest sign of trouble. She also got a great vet tech who allowed her to plow through the line of owners who showed up with their dogs and cats, kept everyone calm, and earned more than the fifty bucks Carrie gave her.

Gravel crunched.

A battered black SUV pulled next to her trailer, screeching to a halt in a cloud of dust. The door popped open and a short, stocky woman slid out. "Are we in time?" She pushed back a strand of lank brown hair which had escaped its messy bun.

"Didn't think we'd get anyone else, but there's still time. How many do you have?"

"One dog. A yellow mutt." She turned to the truck's interior. "She's still open." The engine cut off.

"I'll be inside the trailer. Come on in when you're ready." Though it sent a chill up her spine each time she entered, the A/C brought welcome relief from the heat.

The trailer door opened and the woman entered followed by a man with a large plastic dog crate.

"I'm Carrie Fletcher, the vet."

"I'm Jenna Frances, and this is my husband Larry. We've got Bear with us today."

Frances. A common gargoyle surname, and it matched with the stony vibe they'd given her. "Nice to meet you. Just sign in on the sheet, please. I take it Bear is a male?

"Male." She huffed a humorless laugh. "He's become quite

the asshole and we're thinking neutering is the best thing for him." The two gargoyles shared a smug glance.

"Neutering is always a good thing for dogs." Carrie put some paperwork on a clipboard. "If he continues to exhibit bad behaviors, then you should explore other reasons, like diet, dog companions, or exercise."

This time the two laughed, though they tried to cover it with coughing. Jenna said, "I think this will do the trick and we won't have any more problems with him."

"Okay. If you'll get him up on the table, I'll get ready."

Carrie concentrated on setting out new supplies. Luckily the procedure only took about fifteen minutes once the anesthesia took hold. She turned back to the couple who had placed their dog on the table with care.

"Why is he hogtied?" She could understand the muzzle, but all of his legs were bound as well.

"I told you he was an asshole," Jenna said. "Once you get him under sedation, he'll be fine."

"Alright." Carrie reached for her stethoscope.

"Aren't you going to put him under?"

"Not yet. Since I'm unfamiliar with the patient, I have to do a routine examination first."

"Uh, we're kind of in a hurry. I saw on the internet this should only take about fifteen minutes." She flashed a glance at her husband. "Our son has a, uh, baseball game starting soon."

"This won't take long. And at his age, we should be done in fifteen minutes. But I'll need to observe him to make sure he comes out of the anesthesia well, everything holds, and you've got his medical restrictions. Maybe forty minutes total."

Carrie inserted the stethoscope's tips in her ears and placed the chest piece on his heaving side. Poor thing. Probably scared to death. *I'd be scared if I had these unfeeling gargoyles as my owners.*

Except these weren't the pants of a frightened dog. His breathing was way too labored, as if he had no room for air. And his heart... His heart sounded like the squeeze of a sponge every time it beat. *Crap.* Heartworm? Good chance they didn't give this animal its preventative. Usually she closed off her senses unless needed. Animals often freaked out at the vet's office and panic didn't tell her what she needed to know. She opened the gates.

*No, no, no.* The words reverberated over and over bouncing around in her brain. The energy, warm and authoritative. If she didn't know any better, she'd have thought it... No. Nathan? How could they have made him into an obese seventy-pound lab-mix?

She took a long breath. How to work the code word into a sentence. Then stall. "He's like a pork sausage. You sure he isn't a little piggy? Or does he think he's the Big Bad Wolf?" Hopefully she'd worked the team's code word—'wolf'—for trouble into the conversation without the couple any wiser. She could hang on until the team arrived, right?

"Wolf. Ha, ha. Nope, our little pig." Jenna's tone had grown waspish.

*Hurry up.* She tried to suppress the tremble in her hands as she removed the stethoscope earpieces and hung the device around her neck. She cleared her throat. "Well, he seems to have some trouble breathing and his heart sounds like it's laboring."

"He's probably scared being here." Jenna said.

Carrie nodded her head and tried to slow her speeding heart. "It's not abnormal for them to be scared at the vet's office. And I'm sure the way you have him tied up would freak out most animals." She took a step back and tried to make it look like she hung her hand in her back pocket when she really curled it around her silver sorcerer-spelled folding knife guaranteed to cut through everything. Including stone-hearted gargoyles. "But when I listened to his breathing and heartbeat, it sounds to me like he's got a problem. Most likely heartworm."

"What?" The two looked at each other.

Seconds had ticked by and no team. Where the heck were they? "What preventative do you use?"

"I don't remember," Larry said, anger raising his tone. "We get it at Walmart." Red flooded his gray-tinged face. "He ain't got no heartworm, lady. Do the free surgery like you advertised."

Why would they bring him here instead of killing him outright? To get her to neuter him? Keep stalling. "I need to make sure the animal's healthy before I do anything. If I put a dog with severe heartworms, like it appears this one has, under anesthesia, he could die. Better to get him started on the meds and worry about the neutering later."

Instead of the knife, she pulled a pen from her back pocket, an indestructible steel one she'd gotten from her self-defense trainer for her birthday. Perfect as an unobtrusive weapon, Hannah had said. Carrie clamped down on the crosshatched surface to stop the trembling in her fingers, then picked up her metal clipboard for available follow up appointments. "I'll honor the freebie neuter, but since you said you're short of time, we don't have time for an x-ray. I do home visits. When would you like me to come out?"

Her thoughts spun crazily while her mouth spewed out the right words. Sometimes the most complicated magic could be undone in the simplest means. And transformation spells were notoriously tricky to perform, yet with only a simple word uttered by anyone, the victim could be returned to their true state. Surely it couldn't be that simple? She dug through her memory, but the word she'd learned from her mother eluded her.

The door to the trailer opened. They made it.

MayLee stuck her head in. "Need help?"

*Get her out of here. If they hadn't made it by now, I'm facing this alone.* Maybe the communications link faltered and MayLee could warn them. Carrie schooled her features. "Thanks, though, we're talking through medication options for their little house wolf here."

"Cool. See you tomorrow." She shut the door.

Tomorrow? Hopefully the teen's last odd phrase meant she understood the code word. At least Carrie wouldn't have to worry about the girl getting in the mix. She surveyed the couple across the exam table and her stomach twisted. Her training had been all about personal defense. With the last three years, she could react to an attack, but to do it on her own when Nathan's life could well hang in the balance? Her palms grew slick. *Dang it.* Where was the team?

"Well, then." She gestured with the clipboard. "I guess we'll set up a follow up appointment for you and...Bear?"

"Fuck you, you Leftover bitch." Larry charged around the table.

She whipped the metal clipboard at him like a Frisbee. The hard edge caught him in the throat and he felt back with a gurgle. Jenna came hot on his heels. Carrie got out her knife, but didn't have enough time to flip it open before the gargoyle barreled into her, backed her up against the cabinets. The woman's heavy fist bashed into her stomach. Spots danced in Carrie's vision.

*Don't give up.* Her animals deserved more. Nathan deserved more. She flipped the blade on her knife and drove it into the woman's ribcage at the same time she brought her knee up into her groin.

The scream assaulted her eardrums. She pushed Jenna to the ground, then rushed toward her other opponent.

Larry pulled himself up to regain his feet then fell again as the trailer jolted and started to move forward.

Carrie stayed upright by grabbing the exam table. She kicked the gargoyle in the face and he fell back, dark blood sprayed from his nose and mouth.

The bonds around Nathan's legs were tough, and her hand slipped several times from Jenna's dark gargoyle blood on the knife's handle. The blade finally cut through. A searing pain sliced into the back of her thigh and she screamed in agony. Her head jerked back by a yank of her ponytail as Larry snarled.

She flipped the knife and jabbed it backward, met flesh. She shoved the four-inch blade hard. Then turned her body, bringing the blade with her sideways until it cut free through tough skin.

The gargoyle let go of her ponytail and Carrie staggered forward. She probed the back of her leg and found a good-sized folding knife not unlike her own. Her hands curled around the handle. *No.* her medical side screamed. *Leave it.*

She gritted her teeth against the pain. Her hand found Nathan's forehead. Hopefully she could say it as taught to her by her Clan Magic mother. "Ba-bareshelm." She'd stuttered. Do it again.

The trailer rocked hard and she stumbled, fell into Larry. The knife skittered from her hand, while the knife in her thigh pushed deeper. She screamed as white hot agony arced through her.

His heavy fist cracked on her cheek. The stars came before the pain.

Heaviness dropped on her stomach. Her vision cleared and she found Larry straddling her, arm raised. Her hand sought anything she could use as a weapon. She curled her fingers around a piece of metal—a surgical tool—and she swung at his face. The scalpel wouldn't cut his skin easily, but she'd caught something important.

His nose and eye.

He bellowed and clapped his hand over his face, yet still raised his arm like a hammer.

She tossed the scalpel and fisted her hands, driving them into his groin with every ounce of strength remaining within her.

His fist flew wide of its mark, smashing into the metal cabinet behind her with an audible crunch of stone against steel.

Silver winked in her peripheral. With another rock of the trailer, her blade slid within reach, and she grabbed it. Shoved it in the gargoyle's chest, one hand on the handle, the other driving behind it, adding momentum until the hard, cold skin met the hilt.

"Bitch, I'm gon-gon..." Larry slumped, the blade's magic making short work of his beating heart.

The harsh prickle of electrical tingling made Carrie buck the gargoyle from her then stumble to her feet before the dead gargoyle turned to stone. Each time she moved her leg, the blade still embedded to the hilt in the back of her thigh cut a little more. She'd need to stabilize it to avoid additional damage until it could be removed.

Vibration under her said they were still moving. And at a high rate of speed. The female—Jenna—lay on the other side of the table. Stony, sightless eyes from the granite face confirmed no threat remained.

A jolt pushed Carrie forward to the exam table and she put out a hand to stay upright. She placed her other hand over Nathan's eyes. Took a deep breath to calm her panting and wildly beating heart.

The word had to hold authority. She lowered her lashes, summoned her most commanding voice, the one she used with horses. "Bareshelm."

With the fading of the word, a white glow began to surround Nathan. The pelt began to split, a blinding glare emanating from within, pushing the yellow Labrador retriever coat apart. Carrie shaded her eyes with her arm, unable to bear the brightness.

Within seconds, Nathan's wolf lay on the exam table. Rather, his wolf covered it and then some. He took two huge breaths then slid his front feet to the floor, followed by his rear. The vibration under their feet slowed then ceased. The fur on his shoulders stood on end.

The door opened and Nathan lunged forward.

# CHAPTER 12

Nathan leapt for the door as the handle turned. Fury made up for the exhaustion of being cramped into the size of a Labrador and he hit the door with all the rage of a demon. The door slammed against the side of the trailer and the person opening it fell backward. Nathan landed and wheeled around.

Three beings. One of whom was in the process of picking herself off the pavement. The tall, dark elf from the house and by their smell, the two sorcerers.

Carrie appeared in the trailer's door.

No. She couldn't be harmed again. He couldn't let the sorcerers hurt her. First them, then the elf with his long, lethal blade.

Nathan sprang at the woman, the leader of his transformation, therefore the strongest of the two. He landed on her as she regained her feet, pushing her backward again and clamped down on her throat. Blood spurted into his mouth. Grim satisfaction flowed through him.

A blow sent searing pain into his ribs and moved his body

from standing on hers, but didn't dislodge his fangs. He finished the job with a wrench, then spit her windpipe from his fangs.

He leapt back from a second kick and squared off against the male sorcerer, whose hands cupped a glowing ball of energy. He reared back with the spell.

*This was gonna hurt.* Nathan braced for impact.

A silver flash spun through the air and lodged in the sorcerer's throat, handle deep. Blood leaked from either side where the blade severed both blood vessels. The spell ball fell to the concrete, sizzling.

Nathan scanned to seek the source.

Carrie? She stood in the trailer door, clutching the edges, a smile in her grimace. How could—

Glinting from his right drew his attention away and he dodged left as the elf's lethal blade slid by, ruffling his fur. He snarled and they began a slow circle while they sized each other up. The tall fae weighed a good two-twenty, all lean muscle, and would top Nathan in human form by an inch or two. In his hand, a deadly blade of elf silver created to kill a shifter. The fae had Nathan in size, but Nathan had him with the wolf's faster reaction time. The elf feinted right.

A test only, one Nathan didn't fail. He huffed a laugh then crouched as if to spring.

The elf tensed, but didn't take the bait either.

*Don't have all day.* Help was bound to come, but he couldn't chance it being from the wrong side. He leapt forward.

The elf sidestepped, and swung his blade. Nathan twisted in midair and rolled to his paws, the sword missing him by a bare inch. He sprung to the elf's left side, his weak side. Nathan's fangs locked into the elf's body, teeth skittering along the ribs as he ripped flesh from bone. He received a dizzying blow to his head and retreated beyond the deadly arc.

Blood slicked his opponent's black t-shirt. One to nothing.

The elf became a blur, moving faster than Nathan could dodge. The fae had him by the throat, squeezing off his air. Nathan focused on the sword, poised to strike his soft belly. This was it.

A burst of bright heat rolled over Nathan. The elf screamed and fell back, releasing his captive as fire engulfed him.

Nathan scrambled to his feet and found no one around him. What the hell? He glanced at Carrie whose jaw hung slack as she tracked something in the sky.

An enormous winged creature. For several seconds his brain couldn't function. Then all synapses began firing at once.

A dragon?

Where...? How...? They'd gone extinct over a thousand years ago.

Something moved in his peripheral vision. The elf staggered to his feet, charred and bleeding.

The dragon dove, wings folded back, a massive black arrow of scales and muscle focused in on its target.

No. They needed the elf alive to question. If he could only turn back into human, but his body refused to shift.

A roaring river of superheated magic fire forced Nathan back as it engulfed the elf. There'd be no questioning a crispy husk of former immortal. Or even the possibility of a necromancer compelling information from the dead.

The dragon banked left, then swooped around in a graceful arc. Then headed right back toward Nathan.

His gut clenched. He had no defense for that. *Run.* He must distract it from Carrie.

He looked over his shoulder, but instead of chasing him, the iridescent-scaled monster swooped toward the trailer where Carrie stood.

No. His heart stuttered. He wheeled around and raced back.

Still a hundred feet away from Nathan, its feet came to touch the earth in front of Carrie, wings blowing up an enormous cloud of rusty-colored dust. But the beast lost its balance, then stumbled sideways. It couldn't recover, tumbled to the ground, landed hard on its nose.

He rushed to Carrie, her face streaked with tears. He had to protect her from the monster. He slid between the two, snarling a warning to stay away. Wait. Carrie wasn't crying. She was...laughing? He pushed at her with his side and managed to move her a couple of paces back.

She stumbled, hobbled a bit but managed to remain upright, using one leg and shooting him a fierce grimace.

*Merde.* He'd forgotten about the stab wound to her leg. Watching her fight those gargoyles while he could do nothing nearly killed him. But her injury didn't matter.

He had no weapon for a beast with armored scales hard as diamonds and foot-long, wicked talons. She needed to leave *now* while he covered her escape. More gently this time, he nudged her with his flank.

Carrie chuckled and waved him off with her hand. "It's okay." Her low laughter ceased when he growled at her. "Nathan. Stop. It's MayLee."

MayLee? Who...oh, Barry Montez's great-something granddaughter. He backed up and gazed at the dragon. She'd picked herself up and shook her head as if to bring her senses back.

Carrie limped into the trailer.

The two shifters sized each other up. MayLee? A dragon? Huge, green-blue vertically-slitted pupils stared back through narrowed lids. Perhaps she sensed his skepticism. Her scales rippled and she stretched wide, inky wings that shimmered in the late afternoon sun.

Two could play at the intimidation game, predator to predator. His hackles rose, then he lifted his lip. The low, deadly snarl said he meant business.

She huffed a puff of smoke through her nostrils, clearly not intimidated in the least. Her long, lethal claws dug into the baked earth. She sucked in a huge breath, lifted her head to the sky, opened her maw with its white, deadly teeth.

Nathan braced against the sound.

What should've been a roar of flame became a series of choking gasps.

He chuffed a laugh.

"Will you two knock it off? Geez." Carrie's head poked out of the trailer. "You're both deadly predators, blah, blah, blah." She threaded a pair of jeans and a plaid snap shirt through a grab bar at the side of the door, then sent Nathan a pointed glare. "Come inside, Fido. She needs to shift and get dressed."

He growled his displeasure at the mocking name, but followed her into the trailer anyway.

"Lay down."

He lifted a lip to show the bright white of his fang. How dare she treat him like some lap puppy?

Carrie's brows snapped together. "Stop being a horse's ass and lay down." She pulled a large rolled bandage and some gauze packages from one cabinet drawer, then a black pouch from another. "I hope we can get another one of these." The magic pulsing from the little bag said she wasn't fooling around.

He didn't give his trust in her a second thought and laid on the ground like a good boy.

She gathered the supplies from the counter, then maneuvered to the metal floor next to him with her back against the side wall, tented her injured leg, reached around the limb, and with a violent pull ripped open her jeans. A strangled gasp escaped her.

Carrie held up a syringe, poked the needle into a small bottle and pulled an amount into the cylinder. She poked it into the back of her leg, once, then again, again and again on both sides of the handle sticking from her leg. She rested her head on the trailer wall, then rolled it to face him. "Local anesthesia. This is going to hurt."

A growl ripped from his throat directed at the two gargoyles at the back of the trailer. If he could kill them again, he would. At least the necromancer would have something to work with, though he feared these two were low rungs on the ladder. The sorcerers may provide better information if they could find a necromancer.

A raspy chuckle broke from Carrie. "Down boy." She tore open the rolled bandage's plastic wrapper, opened the packets, and piled two sets of gauze pads. With a deep, unsteady breath, she put the pads on either side of the knife, securing them with one hand. With the other, she began her wrap to steady the blade, holding the beginning awkwardly with the wrist holding the gauze in place. A bare hiss escaped as she rolled the bandage around her leg several times. Finally, she released her other hand and tied it in place. She rested her shaking hands on the floor, her head leaned back against the trailer wall, lids lowered, and lips compressed into a bloodless line.

He knew why she left it in—she couldn't heal like the rest of the paranormal world and its best never to remove an object from a puncture wound. How she fought with the knife in her leg and then performed her own first aid humbled him.

Why hadn't she waited until MayLee had shifted and

changed? Probably to keep the young woman from the diffi-cult task Carrie could perform on herself, even suffering through agony. He marveled at his mate's compassion and selflessness, even while he ached to chastise her for the very same thing. She'd risked all to rescue him and now this. Any man or paranormal being would be lucky to have such a woman.

For several moments, she merely breathed until finally she uttered a shaky laugh. "Well, *that* hurt." Sweat dotted her fore-head above her wan smile. She held up the black pouch. "Somehow I think this may hurt you more though."

Whatever it was, hopefully it allowed him to shift back to his human form. He didn't care how much it hurt.

After loosening the strings, she worked the fabric until it revealed part of a smooth sphere. It hummed with magic. She picked it up by her index finger and thumb without touching the ball directly. "Are you ready?"

He tried to prepare himself, as magic rarely came without a price. Pieces of soul, body, or pain were often the commodities paid for complex spells, sometimes for the doing, sometimes for the undoing, often for both. The instant the orb touched his forehead, pain shot through him, a lightning bolt touching every nerve ending and bathing them with indescribable agony.

Finally, it faded. Nathan sucked for air, heart pounding in his ears, muscles twitching. Over the years, you got used to the shift. The bones shortening or elongating. Muscles and tendons pulling. But this? Blood roared through his veins as he shivered with cold, a probable side-effect of the magic. Whoever did this to him would pay. He clenched his jaw to keep his teeth from chattering.

He pushed up with his hands, then fell back when they

wouldn't hold him up. Well, they'd pay as soon as he could stand.

"Shhh." Carrie stroked his hair. When had she put his head in her lap? "It'll be better in a minute. Rest."

Something light landed over his icy bare skin, lending him the warmth he needed. He cracked an eye. A blue fleece blanket.

She smiled down at him, then reached over and clicked a cabinet door shut.

He spoke through tight, frigid lips. "Wha-what did you mean when you said you ho-hoped you could get another one of these?"

A knock interrupted what would've been a swear-laden response to her story of Suds' predicament.

MayLee popped her head in the door, caution limning her features. "Everyone decent?"

He cleared his throat. "Come on in."

She bounded in the trailer. "Hey, uh..." She looked down at her bare feet and wiggled her toes peeping out from the hem of the jeans. "How did you know it was me?"

"I felt your thoughts and it became pretty clear. And no one I know has eyes your color of teal blue." Carrie gingerly rose to her feet and crossed to MayLee. "Don't worry. We won't say anything."

Nathan did a double take at Carrie's words.

A smile nearly split MayLee's face in two. "Really?" She threw her arms around Carrie.

"What?" Both women swung their attention to him with his exclamation. "Dragons aren't supposed to exist any longer. The Clan would never forgive me for not reporting her. Let alone NAC regulations for an unregistered immortal."

If someone, like a human, didn't know of the paranormal

world then they could remain outside NAC rules. But MayLee came from a registered fae family. For Barry to harbor an unregistered shifter could land him in a world of hurt with the NAC, and put both Nathan and Carrie in the same boat.

"Absolutely. We will not say a word." Carrie shot him a pointed glance over her shoulder that said she'd win any future discussion on the subject. Then she set MayLee at arm's length. "But where did you come from? I thought you were supposed to run to your Grandpa's at the slightest sign of danger?"

"Yeah, well, I saw the fae get into your truck and I just, like, knew they were going to take off, so I rolled into the bed." She hung her head a bit and shrugged, a quintessential chastened teenager, only to puff up again. "But I helped, right?"

"Yes, you helped," Nathan said, finally able to climb to his feet. He secured the blanket around his waist. "But I wanted to keep that elf alive for questioning. If you'd left him for me rather than turning him into a crispy critter, even if he died we could've had a necromancer retrieve his memories. Maybe figure out who's running this show."

The girl's shoulders sagged. "Shoot. I'm sorry. I thought...I thought..." A tear rolled down her cheek.

Carrie's lips compressed to a line which said he'd better fix this.

Oh hell. He crossed to MayLee and slung his arm around her shoulder. "It's okay, kiddo." He pulled her side to his, an awkward pat his only defense against the young woman's tears. "You didn't know."

MayLee sniffed. "Thanks."

His wolf's hearing picked up the hum of an engine sounding in the distance. "We have company."

Carrie put her index finger to her ear. "It's Chip, Uno, and Fuzzy. Barry's with them."

"Uh oh." Horror flooded MayLee's face. "You can't tell Pa-Pa what I did."

Nathan huffed a laugh. "Doncha think you should've thought about that before you turned the elf to a charcoal briquet?"

# CHAPTER 13

T he sunset glowed on Enchanted Rock's face. Carrie sipped her beer from the comfort of the couch where she'd virtually planted herself since returning from the NAC's med ward two days ago. The stitches would come out tomorrow, and the pain had nearly gone. Hell, if she could see them, she'd take them out herself.

She snorted and took another swig. The contortions it would take to get the back of her leg in the mirror would be worth the drive back to the ward. At least the short fae blade missed everything important in her thigh—the femoral, the common peroneal nerve bundle, ligaments, bone... A wonder, surely, that in three days she'd be practically good as new.

With the exception of one thing. They couldn't do anything about a broken heart.

Nathan's crew and Barry had arrived, but only after they'd defeated another set of Elfs and shifters sent in to take them out.

NAC Security flooded the scene hot on the team's heels, then hustled away the shifter enforcers away for debriefing while Carrie went to the Med Ward. She'd seen neither hide nor hair of them since.

Not one call. Not one message.

Probably still being debriefed, her practical side said. But for three days, the sneaky voice of her heart questioned. It made sense. Clan Shifter had been trying to handle the possibility of Garrett Frazier's return on the D-L. It wouldn't sit well with Council politics. Too bad for the shifters.

She'd had her own debriefing, after they'd patched her up and sent her home, of course. Instead, Simon, the silver-haired elf, questioned her, gently but directly. When it came to how the fae ended up a crispy critter, all Carrie would say is she'd been inside the trailer and hadn't seen what happened. The elf probably would've smelled a lie otherwise. Hopefully Nathan had already worked it out with MayLee for her own debriefing. Regardless, Carrie made a promise to the young woman and she wouldn't renege.

After the questioning, Simon told her he would head a team of twenty, dedicating themselves to her safety. The change from Nathan would be for the best. Wallowing in undeclared, miserable love wasn't her style.

She snorted a laugh. Like it already hadn't happened. The downtime with her leg allowed her to loll in unhappiness for the last two days. Stupid girl. How could she love someone who didn't trust her enough he had to make the decisions for her?

But what about how he'd protected her? Fought for her? She tried to shove those traitorous thoughts aside. He should've at least called.

The front door opened, but she didn't bother craning her head to see who entered. Whichever member of the security detail came inside probably needed a bathroom.

Max, however, was bred to master every element in her

surroundings. Usually, she'd chirp a warning woof in their direction. Instead, she pushed to her feet and headed with an easy wag of her feathery tale around the couch and toward the footsteps headed her way. Simon's healing had worked as many wonders for her pup as the NAC's medical personnel had worked on Carrie herself. The border collie bore only a bandage on her ear, a slight limp in her back leg, and the cone's shame for a couple more days. She already didn't seem to be hampered by the single eye.

If Max hadn't sounded off, it meant they were an accepted pack member. And only one person fit the bill besides Carrie. He'd left behind his boots and padded forward on sock feet to stop directly behind the couch.

The scant reflection of Nathan behind her echoed in the plate glass window.

She stared at him staring at her through the medium for several heartbeats. She drank in his features, strong jaw with its hint of scruff, lips with their signature cocky curl nowhere in evidence.

"Beautiful."

The traitorous bump of her heart said she'd have to tread carefully. Best to play it cool. "Yeah, Enchanted Rock is always beautiful this time of day."

"Not the rock. You." His gaze, even in the dim image, held an intensity she didn't want to contemplate.

She swigged the last of her beer and set the bottle on the side table with a snap. "We covered this already. I don't think..."

He rounded the couch to kneel in front of her. "Before you continue, listen to what I have to say. Please." He enfolded her hand in both of his.

The puppy-dog eyes weren't fair. She had no resistance, as he probably well knew. If she opened her mouth she'd encourage him. She settled for frowning and tugging her hand free, then folding her arms across her chest.

She'd heard long ago that hints didn't work on men, as evidenced by Nathan's blithe disregard of her defensive body language.

"I heard you when you said I made the decision without giving you an opportunity. I was a *couillon* for what I did. Any stupider and I shouldn't be able to breathe." He stood and began to pace the length of the large living area. "You deserve someone who knows what he's worth. After Garrett murdered your parents, I felt like a failure and I thought I didn't deserve you. You couldn't possibly want such a failure as a mate." He stopped in the middle of the room.

"Nathan, I—"

"Please, let me finish."

For an alpha to plead... She dipped her chin once.

"I may have felt I wasn't worthy of you, but what I didn't understand is it wasn't my decision to make. I'm sorry I didn't give you the option to decide if you wanted me." A corner of his lips quirked. "Deciding for others is kind of a hazard in the wolf shifter community and a hard habit for an alpha to break. You notice I let you go on your rounds when I wanted you to stay at home, right?"

She leaned forward in her seat, placing her hands on her thighs. He'd gone from apologizing to *that*? "You *let* me go on my rounds?"

He held up his hands as a grimace crossed his features. "Okay. 'Let' was a bad word choice. I understood why you needed to go, despite me not likin' it for tactical reasons."

"How about I went and you had no option but to follow." Oh, the raging egotism.

He tilted his head. "*Chere*, don't think I couldn't have

restrained you. Taken your keys. Locked your gate. If I didn't want you to go, you wouldn't have." She opened her mouth to argue, but he plowed on. "But that's not the point. I couldn't make the decision for you, however much I wanted to. I gave you the reasons why I didn't want you to go, but the decision was yours to make." He spread his hands out at his side. "I'm trying, *bebe*. Can you forgive me for being a stupid, arrogant coon-ass and find it in your heart to—"

"I forgive you." The hope flaring in his eyes made her jump to her feet. She cringed at the stabbing in the back of her thigh, but he had to understand. "That's all it can be. We can't go back to where we were, Nathan. Besides, never once have you said I was your mate. I couldn't handle it if some rando woman showed up and your wolf decided she was the one."

His jaw slackened. "How could you not know you're my mate?" Before she could open her mouth, he answered his own question. "Because I'm a *bibitte* and never told you." He covered his face with his hand.

"Bullshit. You wouldn't have been able to stay away for three years."

"I'm stubborn, or haven't you figured that out yet?" He barked a short, bitter laugh, then his shoulders slumped. "It was hell, Carrie. But I'd convinced myself you were better without a mate who couldn't take care of you." The pain in his words ate at her resolve as it sounded so much like her own. He crossed the short distance to her but his hands dropped to his sides when he would have grasped her shoulders. The restraint poured off of him in waves. "I'm not askin' for us to go back to where we left off. I'm askin' for us to try again. Where we start'll be your decision."

Temptation pulled at her the longer she gazed into his eyes.

Was the soft light in them hope? No. She dropped her regard and wrapped her arms around her middle. "I couldn't stand you leaving again, or you treating me like that again. It would break my heart." Why did she sound as if she contemplated having him back? When had her mind changed from never to maybe? *No, no, no. Back up.* She tipped her head up with a defiant glare. "Besides, you're an alpha, next in line for your pack. What makes you think you'd be able to handle your mate not obeying your every word?"

He raised his hand to cup her cheek and his thumb brushed gently. "I swear, *chere*, I'll do my best, but it's part of my DNA. If I'm actin' like a *tchew*, you remind me I promised. And an alpha always keeps his promises to his pack."

'His *pack*'. The pack was her wavering practicality's answer. She removed his hand from her face, then planted her fists on her hips. " You're the heir of the New Orleans Pack. How am I supposed to fit in? They would never accept an HP as their alpha's mate. I'm sure any females of your pack would gladly mate with you. And your security business is there. I've got my practice *here*." All of those reasons should do it. She muffled her heart's wail.

He shook his head slowly. "Don't you get it yet, *bebe*? Pack leadership means nothin' against the possibility of your love. I can work from anywhere."

A heaviness settled into the pit of her stomach. Oh no. "Shifters are rarely born to HPs. You may be the last of your line." She'd blurted the words, grasping at straws as her resolve started to crumble.

He took one of her hands in his, brushed the back of it with his thumb in a soothing manner. "I know that, but we will be blessed if the Gods grace us with children." A crooked smile crossed his face. "You should remember we mate for life. My wolf and I agree it's you or no other." She opened her mouth to protest, but he put a finger across her lips. "I told my father today he may need to find a new heir. My crew is more than enough to keep an alpha busy."

"*May* need to find a new heir?"

"It depended on how this went." His tone dropped to sexy-ville.

She didn't know how it happened, why it happened, but he'd carved a hole in the dam. Her heart burst, flooding her with hope, drowning out any remaining caution. She snaked her arms around his neck and pulled him close. Instead of a kiss, her nose and forehead met his. She stared deep into the blue flame of his eyes. "You better not make me regret this."

"Never."

The amount of promise in the one word proved to be the death knell for her doubts. "Then the next step should be to kiss and make up, right?"

"Umm-hmm."

For long moments they stared at each other, then she realized he deliberately didn't take the initiative and wanted her to make the first move. Her heart began to canter. She contemplated the sensual curl of his lips. He knew how he affected her, damn him. Maybe it was time he knew how much *she* still affected *him*.

She threaded her fingers through the thick hair at his nape. *Skritched* her short nails against his skin, then pulled his head to her, fitted her lips to his but couldn't stop the little sigh that escaped. She kissed him, nipped a bit at his lower lip, then swept her tongue across, demanding entry.

With a groan, he gave up all pretense of submission. His hands found her butt and hauled her to him, lips parted and they shared the havens of each other's mouths in a duel to see who could give the other the most pleasure.

How she missed this, his mouth, his arms, hands, his animal heat. She moaned into his mouth at the sheer carnality of the kiss.

A chuckle rumbled against her lips, then he redoubled his efforts, his fingers squeezing and massaging her bottom, pulling her up against his erection.

She rocked against his hardness and he growled with need. Now it was her turn to chuckle. *She* did that to him.

His lips roamed from her mouth, strayed down her neck, nipped, laved. Her shirt's hem lifted and his hands swept under, one across her back, the other leaving a hot trail up her ribcage. Her nipples hardened, craving his touch. She moaned as his fingers covered...

A very audible throat clearing broke through to Carrie's consciousness. She froze. Fire bloomed in her cheeks as she tried to rein in her heart's wild gallop, the frantic heaving of her chest. Nathan turned to shield her and she buried her nose in his chest, unwilling to meet anyone's eyes until she could regain control. She smoothed down her shirt, then snuggled against him. Underneath her ear his pulse drummed a rapid beat no less frantic than hers.

"Yes?" The clipped tones of the single word screamed controlled irritation.

"We're ready to roll, boss." Fuzzy's sheepish voice came from over her shoulder.

"Unless you're giving us a well-deserved two-week vacation," Chip added, suggestive laughter bright in her words, something Carrie never would've thought the tough woman could manage.

"Fuzzy can take two weeks. In fact, he can take four." Nathan dropped one arm and curled Carrie into his side, allowing her to view the exchange.

"What about me? I don't get a vacay?" Chip's tone tightened.

"You should've checked your voicemail."

"Can barely get reception around here." She whipped out her phone and started jabbing at the screen.

"Meet with Simon deVrys, Alannah's Detail Leader. He needs you at NAC Security ASAFP."

Her mouth hung open for a moment before she shut it with a snap. "How come—"

"The fae didn't say. What he did say was he needed the best." Nathan lifted his shoulders. "And you're the best."

"Does this have to do with the Pure Paranormal conspiracy and who's behind it?" A spark lit in her eyes.

Nathan shook his head. "He wouldn't say. But if it was my guess, it has to do with the body from Barry's shed." Nathan turned to Carrie with a wolfish grin sliding across his chiseled face. "All I know for sure is I'm in charge of keeping Carrie safe. And I'm gonna make sure I'm dedicated to it." His head dipped and he captured her mouth in a searing kiss Carrie never wanted to end.

When Nathan's head lifted, she was dizzy with desire and the two of them were alone. He swung her up into his arms. "I'm givin' myself four weeks off. I've got three years to make up for."

She wound her arms around his neck. Her heart stuttered at the wicked love shining in his eyes. "Going to try to cram three years in four weeks, eh?" She nuzzled his neck, where his pulse beat strong.

"Bebe, ain't no tryin' to it. I'm gonna do it." A fire in his eyes blazed sensual promise. "Hope you got a lot of that quinoa-stuff. We aren't leavin' here until I've more than made up for my stupidity. I love you chere."

His mouth covered hers in a scorching kiss leaving Carrie no doubt in her mate.

*The Demon's Shifter Mate*
**An Enchanted Rock Immortals Novella**
**by Amanda Reid**
**Coming September 1, 2020!**

**Sometimes you have to break the rules for love...**

Calum Stavros is a man who lives by the rules. As North American Council Security Director, he has a whole manual of regulations to fit every situation, including one forbidding relationships between manager and employee. But rules don't seem to apply to the beautiful and brash wolf shifter Chip Foster, on loan to the agency for a sensitive investigation threatening to bring down the council. She's scented his secret, and now she could bring him down, too.

After a grueling case, tracker extraordinaire Moonlight Lily "Chip" Foster should've been sunning herself on a beach, margarita in hand. Instead, she's in a place she never wanted to be—Enchanted Rock, home of the stuffed-shirt bureaucrats, just like strait-laced Director Stavros. Following the rules has never been her style, but if she does, she can continue tracking what seems to be the impossible rise of a fanatic threatening the paranormal world. Now, if only she could keep her nose on the trail, rather than sniffing around the handsome Director...

*Avian*
## An Enchanted Rock Immortals Novella
### by Eve Cole
### Coming August 4, 2020!

Avian shifter Grayson Harpya is the natural choice for Clan Shifter's next representative to the North American Council. Arriving late and missing the swearing in ceremony isn't the plan. Forgiving the man responsible? Not on the agenda, either.

When Isaac Williams inherited his grandfather's small of plot land near Enchanted Rock, he didn't expect to see the odd assortment of non-native birds flying through. Now's he's accidentally injured a harpy eagle. He tries to nurse the gorgeous, giant bird of prey back to health only to find himself part of a fantastic world he didn't know existed.

Eve Cole's Avian is the first Clan Shifter novella in the Enchanted Rock Immortals series.

# ACKNOWLEDGMENTS

The Enchanted Rock Immortals novella series started, as many good writing ideas do, at a retreat attended by Fenley Grant, Eve Cole, Robin Lynn, Susan Person and I. It might have been the wine, because I can't remember who brought it up, but we kicked it around for a couple of months before realizing the novella concept would be a good fit for all of us since we all are voracious readers of Urban Fantasy Romance. I could say, 'And here we are with you having just read the first in the series', but that wouldn't quite be the case.

It took far more than just writing a story. We all worked in managing a clan—how each of them govern themselves, the "rules" for each of their paranormal abilities, and other tiny details which contribute to the rich paranormal world of the Enchanted Rock Vortex. Fenley (our Grammar Queen) managed the editing; Susan ("I ain't skeert of no interweb") put together our website; and Eve herded cats by gathering everyone's considerable cover opinions to mediate a cover that rocks. Me? I just managed the formatting and uploading of the box set.

I'd like to lift a glass to toast my sisters in the ERI world for all of their hard work, compromise, nail biting and sheer dedication to this project. We did it. And I still love y'all!

# ABOUT THE AUTHOR

Amanda Reid is an author in the Enchanted Rock Immortals world of urban fantasy romance novellas. She also authors The Flannigan Sisters Mysteries, a series of light paranormal cozy mystery novellas.

Since she was young, she's been a lover of mystery, sci-fi, and paranormal books. Amanda found her first romance book in her aunt's closet around thirteen years of age and quickly decided it needed to be added to her repertoire. As do many readers, she'd always dreamed of writing. She finally learned the secret, and she'll let you in on it--do it. That simple.

Beyond writing, Amanda was a career Army brat and lived in exotic locations like Tehran, Iran and DeRidder, Louisiana as a child. She obtained an International Politics degree and dreamed of a career in the State Department, but ended up as a federal agent. Amanda spent 24 years investigating murders, fraud, identity theft, drug dealers and many other crimes before her retirement. As you can imagine, it's given her a wealth of inspiration for her mystery and urban fantasy stories.

She currently lives in Texas with her husband and two gonzo Australian Shepherds. Catch up with her on Twitter or Facebook. You can sign up for upcoming releases and promos at amandareidauthor.com.

Enchanted
Rock
Immortals

Made in the USA
Columbia, SC
12 November 2024

46295135R00081